MARK JULIAN VAMPIRE P.I.
The Case of the Strega's Touch

First Edition

Published by The Nazca Plains Corporation
Las Vegas, Nevada
2009

ISBN: 978-1-935509-51-6

Published by

The Nazca Plains Corporation ®
4640 Paradise Rd, Suite 141
Las Vegas NV 89109-8000

© 2009 by The Nazca Plains Corporation. All rights reserved.
No part of this work may be reproduced or utilized in any form or by any means, electronic or mechanical, including photocopying, microfilm, and recording, or by any information storage and retrieval system, without permission in writing from the publisher.

PUBLISHER'S NOTE
Mark Julian Vampire P.I.: The Case of the Strega's Touch is a work of fiction created wholly by *Kyle Cicero's* imagination. All characters are fictional and any resemblance to any persons living or deceased is purely by accident. No portion of this book reflects any real person or events.

Male Cover Photo, Ronny Thiele
New York - Brooklyn Bridge Photo, Janis Lacis
Art Director, Blake Stephens

DEDICATION

To my friends and family. In particular I note Joe Op. who answered my queries about needles and herbs. To Jesse G. and a huge nod to Tia H. who provided a sense of literacy to my Julian books. To Simon Dex for providing me with the inspiration for the character of Jean-Claude. A huge nod to our long gone neighborhood movie house where I gleefully spent many of my childhood Saturday afternoons watching horror films at their matinees. A final heads up to ***ReVamp*** located in L.A and their limited edition fashion recreations that gave me my ideas for Jaime.

But most of all to my amazing mother who shared with me a love of old fashioned murder mysteries and who always told me I could do anything.

STREGA |ˈsträgə|:

A kind of orange-flavored Italian liqueur.
ORIGINS: Italian, literally a 'witch.'

MARK JULIAN VAMPIRE P.I.

The Case of the Strega's Touch

First Edition

Kyle Cicero

CONTENTS

THE CASE OF THE STREGA'S TOUCH   1

   PROLOGUE   1

   A PROWL IN CENTRAL PARK   5

   A RELATIVE'S VISIT   11

   THAT NIGHT IN THEIR BED   21

   INVESTIGATIONS AND CONFRONTATIONS   31

   PRECINCT DETOURS   35

   ANOTHER REQUEST NOT TO BE DENIED   41

   HAPPENINGS IN THREE PLACES AT THE SAME TIME   51

TWO VISITS TO TWO PARKS	63
WHILE IN ANOTHER DARK PLACE	75
A MEETING AND MUSINGS	79
CONFERENCES AND REALIZATIONS	87
THE DARK TIMES ARE RETOLD	91
A CASTLE WITH A DAMSEL, HER WEREWOLF AND A STREGA	103
SIX MONTHS LATER	115
THE CASE THAT MARKED THE BEGINNING	**121**
LONDON, CLOSE TO THE TURN OF THE NINETEENTH CENTURY	123
THE MEETING	129
THE INVESTIGATION	135
A CONFRONTATION	141
AN ENDING THAT MARKED A BEGINNING	147
THE PANICKY CASE OF THE CUCCIOLO DI LUPO	**153**
ABOUT THE AUTHOR	**161**

THE CASE OF THE STREGA'S TOUCH

PROLOGUE

Marcus Claudius Marcellus had been born in what was later designated as 45 B.C., though historians wrongly cited the date of 42 B.C. He was the only son of Octavia, the daughter of Gaius Octavius, an honest but relatively unimportant man who had the luck of being related to Gaius Julius Caesar through his wife Julia. Gaius Octavius later had a son, also named Gaius Octavius, who was adopted by his soon to be illustrious Uncle Julius and rise up to become known to history as Augustus, the First Citizen Of Rome. Marcus had become a young man with a very bright future indeed!

When his Uncle Octavius, aka Augustus, later had his own daughter Julia wed to Marcus things only improved for him. To everyone this marriage signaled that he was the appointed heir to Augustus' ranks and offices when the latter expired. One day he would become the First Citizen of Rome!

Marcus had loved Julia in his own manner quite intensely and she had indulgently understood that the objects of his primary sexual arousals were always of the more masculine variety. In those days there was none of that latter day Christian narrow-minded judgmental morality concerning whom one slept with so his tastes in bedmates were never a real problem, especially since Marcus was carefully discrete to avoid any gossip that would embarrass his young wife. In their own fashion the two were deeply devoted to each other.

The people of Rome had taken the strikingly good-looking young couple to their hearts and life was good. In truth, the pair had been quite happy until that night in 23 B.C. when Marcus and Augustus were attacked by two vampires hired by practitioners of the dark arts who were angered by Augustus' order that all such persons were to be exiled from Rome. Luckily the first citizen had escaped unhurt but Marcus had not been as fortunate. Though not killed, he had been unintentionally "turned" by his attacker instead. He awoke from his assault to find himself as one of the vampire clan.

Augustus had been grief stricken over this calamity but rigidly firm. It was to be understood by Marcus that a vampire, especially an immortal one, was not a proper heir for the Roman people. Marcus left into a bitter exile while the people were told their darling young future heir had died from an undisclosed illness. Julia remained locked into a loveless second marriage to an old man she despised. After that man's death and Augustus' own demise, her third husband, the Emperor Tiberius, had her killed.

Marcus wandered the earth, ultimately arriving in the New World over a century ago where he now claimed a new city as his home. New York City was a place that reminded him of his old Rome with its whirling brashness, its excitement and, its defiant attitudes toward all comers. Here one could and did become anything they wanted to be or to be *known as, and so Marcus Claudius Marcellus became just simply Mark Julian, remembering his wife in his new life by adopting a form of her first name as his last one. Here he began his new career as an investigator for the supernatural denizens of "his city". Together with his trusty secretary Jaime, shape-shifting sex demon with a dress code straight out the forties, he stood ready to take on all cases that came his way!*

A Boner Book

A PROWL IN CENTRAL PARK

Jean-Claude hurried across town toward one of the less traveled upper sections of the North End of New York City's Central Park. The full moon was rising soon and he wanted to be sure he was hidden in the dense brush and trees of that part of the Loch Ravine area not usually frequented by people during the day, let alone during the hours of darkness. It was the last night of the full moon and Jean-Claude was determined to spend it outdoors and not, as in the previous nights, locked up in the panic room of his Upper East Side condo.

"That damned son-of-a-bitch Tortego," he muttered as he briskly walked through passing crowds, never noticing the looks of sexual interest that were being directed toward him by quite a few men and women who wondered who this impossible handsome dark haired young man was and how they could meet him in a more intimate setting. For now, had disappeared behind the various trees of oak, hickory, maple and ash. To his shock, as he passed through the arch he found not more forest but the manmade Lasker Pool complex. Cursing his forgetfulness about this structure's presence, he doubled back under the arch heading deeper into the North Woods section of the park. Time was critical now but at last he felt he was safe from prying eyes. He moved silently off the path and into the darkness of the northwest slope's forested canopy. He found a quiet secluded place and disrobed. After making sure his suit clothes and other possessions were securely hidden from accidental discovery, Jean-Claude stood naked in the cool night air, letting the sounds of the forest surround his leanly muscled six-foot frame. The change was coming on stronger now and his classically featured face was shifting in its appearance. He crouched on all fours, ready to become one with nature as his green eyes sparkled in the reflected moonlight. Jean-Claude felt his senses reach out into the wildness around him. The excitement of it all caused him to experience a complete sexually arousal. It was then, right in the midst of his transformation, he felt the presence of someone else…someone who was human! By now his metamorphosis was too far-gone for him to act. The effects of converting into what he was becoming had temporarily paralyzed his body's ability to move. Until he fully completed the process that had just initiated he was helpless to flee or defend himself. He growled, hoping the angry noise would scare off the person he now knew was rapidly closing in upon him. Just a few more minutes, he thought, and he would be transformed and capable of moving further away into the safety of the nighttime forests. His mind suddenly exploded, signaling the final stages of his biological progression. He was once more his other half: a true wolf of the Roué clan. Instinctively, he howled into the night with his joy. He was ready to move to safety.

Suddenly a sharp crack broke through the night's silence. His side felt a sharp jab as if he had been stung. Turning his head to the source of the pain, he observed that some type of feathered dart had hit him. The thought that anyone would dare to strike at him enraged him. Emitting a low growl he turned toward the dart's source to defend himself from another such assault. His heart increased its beating while his lean and sleekly muscled wolf's body tensed for attack. Little did he know that his rage only aided the liquid that that the dart had injected inside of him. With a loud roar he signaled his readiness to face his attacker, still hoping his actions would scare the human off, thus avoiding any needless bloodshed. He was not only a wolf of the Roué clan; he was the designated crown prince of the clan, as well. He would fight to kill if he had to but, like all of his kind, would only kill a human if necessary for his own safety. He sensed the human waiting close by. A few seconds later an unexpected dizziness overcame him. His powerful wolf's body slunk helplessly downward until he lay sideways on the forest's matting of wet undergrowth. Everything grew hazy by then. He barely sensed the approaching human. After a few minutes, as if from a great distance off, he heard the voices of at least four humans. His last conscious sensation was that of his body being gently hoisted up and carried off.

A Boner Book

A RELATIVE'S VISIT

Mark Julian, New York City's premier vampire private detective for the supernatural community, was currently in his office at his desk, busily reviewing the agency's latest expense accounts. Outside, the blare of traffic horns and the busy commercial life on nearby Delancey Street in the Lower East Side carried on at its usual brassy New York City pace. As he gazed dumfounded at the agency's bills, he loosened his tie and gasped at what he saw. "Jaime," he yelled as he saw his secretary's latest set of billing expenses. "Get in here now!"

"Problem, boss," Jaime said as she sashayed in from her desk in the outer office. "Oh," Jaime replied as she (*for today the shape-shifting sex demon was in her feminine form so, the use of the feminine pronoun was the order of the day when referring to "her"*) observed the look of growing annoyance play itself out on Mark's face. "I see the clothing store's bill just came in. You said I could replace the outfit that was slimed by the sewer demon during our last case when I helped on the stakeout."

"Is that what **Retro for the Hetro** is…a clothing store?" Mark grumbled as he glanced over the second page of itemized bill. "Sweet Venus, what the hell did you buy there for…Jaime it's over $1785!" He yelped as he gazed up at his secretary with a look of shock and horror.

"Gees Mark, its not easy finding vintage clothes from the forties!" Jaime responded as she adjusted her well-tailored, light blue long sleeved jacket, which she had combined with a matching pair of high-waist pants that was "all the rage" in nineteen forty-three. "I mean a girl…or a boy," Jaime slyly added with a wink, "well, *one* has to go either to one of the outer boroughs nowadays to find just the right ensemble or order direct from a rather nifty store out in Los Angeles."

The twenty-two year old (*if one counted only the years he was alive as opposed to being undead*) detective was rendered speechless. At that moment however, he decided on two things: 1) never employ Jaime as a lookout on any future case no matter how hard she/he begged and, 2) never promise to replace any of Jaime's clothes! He was just about to suggest that Jaime dress more in the latest fashions of this millennium when he heard the outer door open.

"Oh, I forgot you have a client," Jaime quickly said as a sly grin came across her attractive face. Her sea green eyes took on a mischievous glimmer. "I will just show them in, boss," she chuckled as she adjusted the hair net holding her golden-flecked brown hair. She turned and rushed toward the outer office. "Hello," Mark heard her say. "He is absolutely waiting to see you. Yes, he loves seeing you too."

Mark was completely at a loss to figure out with whom his appointment was with. In fact, until this moment, he wasn't even aware he even had an appointment. He nearly went into shock when in walked Vinnie's mother, accompanied by another woman. "Mrs. Pasquale," he sputtered while shooting Jaime a look which said '*you die I swear it*'. He rose from his chair and went around to the smiling woman who always expected a hug from him and kiss on the cheek whenever he greeted or left her.

Mark had first met, and locked horns with, homicide detective Vinnie Pasquale when the PI was hired by the head of the New York City's supernatural council to secretly investigate killings by a rogue vampire. Vinnie, a then thirty year old New York law officer, had also been officially assigned to solve the case the city's press had dubbed "The Choirboy Killer". They had clashed from the start with Vinnie resenting interference by a private investigator in an official police matter and Mark resenting the former's presence in his hunt for the killer. By the end of the case each had not only grown to respect the other but, to their mutual surprise, they had also fallen in love with each other. For Mark, finding himself to be truly in love with a human was amazing. For Vinnie, who until this time had been engaged to a woman, discovering he was attracted to a man who was also a vampire, as well, had been an unsettling revelation. Telling his old fashioned Italian family he was gay and dating Mark had been even more unsettling a prospect. Vinnie's mom, however, brought them all around. Vincenzo was her cherished "baby boy" and nothing he did or whom he dated mattered for her as long as he was happy. And so, Mark found himself pulled into Vinnie's human family and the dominating presence of their matriarch.

"Mark," the diminutive four foot ten inch white haired Italian woman said with obvious joy. "Meet my old friend Teresa Castillo."

Mark smiled and nodded at the woman only to find himself swept up into an embrace by Mrs. Castillo. Unlike Vinnie's mother, Mrs. Castillo, though taller, was barely five foot one. She was also a good deal heavier. Vinnie's mom probably weighed no more than ninety-eight pounds while Mrs. Castillo looked to be at least double that weight. Yet both women, it seemed, did share a few things in common, namely a warm engaging smile that was combined with a very exuberant personality. Inspite of his apprehension at their visit, Mark couldn't help but smile seeing these two older women all dressed up in their Sunday best, complete with hat and gloves, clearly excited to be seeing him. For a brief second he saw in each of them the excited entrancing young girls they must have been over seventy years ago.

"Vinnie's mother told me how you and her son are getting married soon, so I thought, with my problem, why not give business to family," Mrs. Castillo gushed as Vinnie's mom nodded knowingly.

As her words sunk in Mark felt another tremor of shock. He glanced at Jaime who was barely able to stop herself from laughing out loud. "Vinnie…I…married?" He managed to croak.

"Oh Teresa, I told you they don't want to make a big thing out of it," Mrs. Pasquale chuckled. "But I've spoken to my cousin the priest over at Saint Rocco's, and he will do the ceremony at my house when they pick the date."

By now Mark's head was spinning. "Date…priest. Can't they…I mean doesn't the Pope forbid," he babbled, trying to stop this moving train.

"Oh no one pays attention to that pope,' Mrs. Pasquale said sternly.

"That's right," Mrs. Castillo, agreed. "Besides, who listens to a German pope, and a former Nazi to boot, or so I'm told," she responded forcefully. Mrs. Pasquale tapped the side of her nose with a finger and then sagely nodded, using the universal Italian signal indicating the former was secret knowledge by everyone and her agreement with those facts. "They make such a handsome couple too, Maria," Mrs. Castillo gushed. "Oh, if I had your blue eyes, Mark, when I was a girl," she sighed as she gazed off to one side, lost in memories.

Mark was completely lost in silence by now. Luckily Jaime saw this and took over. "I think we ought to tell Mark what you need him for," Jaime cooed lightly as she guided the women to the chairs in front of Mark's desk while Mark drifted back behind his desk to sit down.

"Such a sweet girl, so trim a figure and you are only twenty-one, I'm told. Single, too, Vinnie informed me." Mrs. Pasquale said smilingly as the women sat. "And you dress so nicely, doesn't she Teresa?"

"Oh yes," Teresa agreed, as she fished out a photo from he pocketbook. "My Charles is single too. He is in the Marines and he is twenty-two. He's home on leave right now, in fact," she continued saying as she passed the picture to Jaime. "By the way, I love how you've set up your hair in that net, dear. Reminds me of how we did it in the war. Remember, Maria," Mrs. Castillo sighed.

Jaime politely took the photo and examined it, giving the image a nod followed by a look that displayed real interest on her part. "He's really striking in uniform, too. Here Mark, take a gander." Jaime stated with amusement as she passed the picture of a quite handsome, well-built, brown haired young man in his dress Marine attire.

"Very nice." Mark said, still coming to grips with what had just been said before by the two women.

"I've met your brother, dear, as well," Mrs. Pasquale continued. "He looks just like you, too. Just as sweet. I've a young cousin he might like to date."

Mark glanced at Jaime, "*If only Mrs. Pasquale knew it was the same person,*" he silently thought before quickly deciding he needed to interject a new topic before he had to explain to Vinnie how he let his mom hook his young female cousin up with a sex demon. True, Jaime preferred men but Vinnie would hardly take comfort in that knowledge if the two went out. As for Mrs. Castillo's young buff boy, well, he was a Marine so he was on his own! "The case, ladies." He blurted out loudly with more force than he intended.

The two women now took on a serious demeanor. Mrs. Castillo suddenly became emotional. "I need you," she managed to say before bursting into tears.

Mark turned his head to Vinnie's mom in panic. Was this breakdown his fault for how he had just spoken to them? Before he could ask this, however, Mrs. Pasquale signaled Mark to not speak. Gently she handed her friend a tissue then looked over at Mark. "We need you to find out who killed …no murdered …her dog!"

Mark glared again at Jaime who shrugged her shoulders feigning, without success, her complete ignorance of any prior knowledge of why they had come to see Mark. "You want me to find a…" he muttered before lapsing into silence.

"A cold blooded bastard killer! I know you will help us! I told my best friend Teresa, that we can count on my future son-in-law to find this no good son-of-a-bitch!" Mrs. Pasquale stated firmly as her friend, with tears still flowing, silently nodded.

"Your future son-in-law," Mark hoarsely repeated.

Jaime put her hand over her mouth and left, shaking in silent mirth at the thoughts that must be racing throughout Mark's mind right now over his surprising engagement. She also knew Mark was completely lost when women cried in front of him.

"The poor girl. We upset her, Teresa," Vinnie's mom sighed sympathetically as Mark sat before them thinking the concern was being directed to the wrong person. "Someone took Teresa's Labrador from her front yard. No one saw it being done. Two days ago they found his –" Vinnie's mom paused, then looked at her friend in concern. "Well, his body was found by a pedestrian pathway in a wooded area along the border of Highbridge Park. The poor animal was still wearing his collar and dog tags so they were able to contact Teresa when he was discovered. Teresa's son went to claim the body and he was told the dog had been mutilated." Mrs. Castillo, having heard those final words, broke down completely while her friend put her arm around her to give her comfort.

"I understand her distress," a shaken Mark said, surprised both at Vinnie's mom's vehemence and by her language. He could appreciate her and her friend's feelings. Hurting animals had always appalled him, but trying to find who kidnapped her dog and then killed it was hardly in his line of work. He was about to tell them both this fact when he saw Mrs. Pasquale's grief stricken face.

"I need you to do this for me." Mrs. Pasquale, somehow anticipating his reply, said softly to him in a way that carried with it both a plea and a command for his assistance.

"Let…can we go over the facts of the…of the…" his voice trailed off in the face of Mrs. Castillo's loud sobs.

"Homicide," Mrs. Pasquale stated with conviction.

Mark nodded. "Jaime, will you come in to take notes please," Mark called out lightly, thinking this was all some bizarre dream or at least hoping it truly was just that. "I should have an answer of some sort in a few days so you can feel free call me then." A half an hour later a flummoxed Mark watched as Jaime escorted the two women out of his office.

"You know this was my first visit to a private investigator's office, dear," he heard Mrs. Castillo say to her friend as they passed through Jaime's outer room. "The entire place looks just like that Bogart movie. You know, the one with that big bird," she giggled as Jaime closed the outer office door behind them.

Mark shook his head, amazed at the surprising turn of events his life had once more taken. If someone had told him over two years ago that he, a vampire, would be in a serious committed relationship with a human, he would have laughed. Even more shocking, the woman had told her friend that Mark and her son Vinnie would be getting married very soon. He could hardly believe the words "soon to be married to my son" in the near future were being used with reference him. Worse, he realized just what he had promised to undertake as a favor to his lover's mother!

"Jupiter Best and Greatest," he blurted out loud after a few minutes. "I'm investigating the killing of a dog!"

"Mother-in-law problems, boss," Jaime's voice called out from her outer room as the sounds of her typing up the interview notes filled the office. The sex demon suddenly stopped her typing and sauntered in wearing a huge grin. "Ah, one's future relatives can be trying, boss."

"You are enjoying this, huh?" Mark groused as he stared at Jaime in annoyance. "And she is not my mother-in-law!"

"Me enjoying your distress, boss," Jaime answered putting on an innocent expression that was so faked it was maddening. "As for the in-law part, she will be rather soon if I heard correctly."

"Jaime!" Mark stated sharply in protest.

"Can I be in the wedding party, boss?" Jaime asked plaintively. "I've always dreamed of wearing this nifty bridesmaid outfit, circa nineteen forty-seven, that I found at the flea market in Chelsea! It's bright red with this pleated hem along the bottom of the skirt..." Jaime prattled on, truly having the time of her life now as Mark seethed.

"Well, you could never wear white so I guess a forty's bridal outfit is out," Mark shot back in annoyance.

Jaime flashed a look of mock horror, then turned and strode out of Mark's office. A few seconds later the CD player by Jaime's desk was playing the Andrew Sister's singing, "I'll be with you in apple blossom time!"

"I'll kill her," Mark moaned as he ran his fingers through his sandy blonde hair. Suddenly he realized that this was the exact same thing Vinnie did whenever he was frustrated. "For the love of Hera, I'm imitating him now." Mark gasped as he grabbed his hat and swept out of the office to walk off his frustrations. "Finish typing up the report and check around to see what you can find from any city agency that might have gotten involved in this situation," he barked at Jaime. "I'll come back later to read it all."

As he waited for the elevator he heard the song "How much is that doggie in the window," emanating from his office. "JAIME I SWEAR!" He roared as he stepped into the just arrived elevator and hit the down button. For the rest of the day Mark Julian, once the celebrated private eye to the supernatural community, found himself beginning the process of investigating the killing of a dog.

A Boner Book

THAT NIGHT IN THEIR BED

For Mark it had been a long day. He had reached out to his usual "supernatural contacts" and asked them to check around to determine if anyone knew anything about the kidnapping or the killing itself. He had endured their varied mocking reactions with a patience he never knew he had possessed. Later, he came back to the office and read the interview notes and other background information Jaime had complied while pondering how much he currently hated his life right now.

It seemed Mrs. Castillo's Lab had been an albino and, because of that rarity, both her and her dog had been written up in one of the smaller local neighborhood papers. The story had soon been picked up for the human-interest sections of the bigger city papers, as well. Mark figured this publicity must have attracted the person who took the animal but Mark was unsure why the killing had taken place. There had to be some logical rationale for it, he thought, but right now it was all just a blank page. He needed more information to fill in the spaces. He ultimately decided to go home and start fresh the next day. That night a tired vampire PI eased himself next to Vinnie in their bed. As usual, Vinnie moved up behind Mark and hugged him close. Feeling the warmth of his lover's powerful body spooning against his own eased the tensions in his torso.

"About time you came home. The bed is always too cold without you," Vinnie murmured with a yawn as he kissed Mark's bare shoulder. "Besides, you know how I hate falling asleep without you beside me in our bed," he muttered as he let his cheek rest on Mark's shoulder.

"*Our bed*," Mark thought to himself enjoying the words as they replayed in his mind. They had recently decided to live together to end the hassle of deciding who was staying over and where that would be. In spite of its smaller size, Mark had happily agreed to transfer his belongings into Vinnie's apartment in the East Village off Tompkins Square Park and to sublet his own Battery Park condo, figuring Vinnie's dwelling was more convenient to the latter's job and his own PI offices in Manhattan's once run down, but currently rapidly gentrifying, Lower East Side. One strong deciding point was that their home, being closer to Vinnie's precinct, would enable him to arrive home faster to Mark whenever the New York City homicide detective finished his irregular shifts. Besides, Mark never felt any attachment to his dwelling there so "moving" for him was never an issue. The new roomier bed they bought had been their first major purchase as a couple. Thinking about their bed brought back memories from over a year ago. Mark remembered with amusement the first time Vinnie slept over at his place.

"Mark," Vinnie had asked hesitantly, "you do have ...a...well," he stopped and gazed at Mark with anxiety. "Well...you do have...a bed right?" He finally blurted out.

Mark had been puzzled for a few seconds before it hit him. "You think I sleep in a coffin. I bet you even think I have some of my graveyard dirt inside it like in the movies," he roared in laughter as Vinnie turned beet red. *"Oh Jupiter Best and Greatest, you do think that too,"* Mark howled, invoking his ancient chief god to witness the site of the blushing young hunk's embarrassment. *"Vinnie, you are so cute when you stereotype vampires like that! I truly have to further educate you on certain things, I guess,"* he concluded as he took Vinnie's hand and led him to the bedroom that contained a bed Mark had acquired from Macy's.

During their first case together the good looking New York City detective had been patiently instructed by Mark on how all the old clichés concerning vampires and crosses, garlic, mirrors, and especially the effects of daylight, went by the boards.

"Look Vinnie, try to forget the Bram Stoker nonsense," Mark patiently explained. *"He was a writer we hired to spread that false information so we'd be safe existing among humans. Not a shred of real truth ...well, perhaps a bit actually...but most of his book is a well crafted tissue of false facts."*

"You mean you guys purposely used him to spread disinformation?" Vinnie had asked in amazement. *"You encouraged him to lie!"*

"I'd rather think of it as a policy of romancing the true circumstances about us to accomplish a greater good, i.e. our survival. Sort of an early version of what certain former United States Presidents now do," Mark replied with a smile. *"I mean, if you believe that vampires cannot live in sunlight and you see me out and about on a sunny day..."* he responded with a smile.

"Then you cannot be a vampire," Vinnie finished the sentence as the logic of this tactic struck home.

Dating and later living with a vampire as one's lover, however, was a whole other story. Over time Vinnie slowly grew comfortable with the idea that vampires were just "regular people" who drank blood, had exceptional strength, and lived forever. True, with regard to prolonged exposure to the sun vampires tended to burn rather than tan, so beach trips were out. It was also true Mark, when he went into what he referred to as his *vampire mode*, needed to both feed and sleep a bit more after extremely strenuous physical activities. On the whole, Vinnie found the few adjustments he made similar to those any new couple made when they set up joint living arrangements. That first year was tricky, and after a slight mishap Vinnie now always remembered that the wine bottles in the back of the fridge did not contain red wine for use in making sauce. Living in a relationship with a human was also daunting for Mark who had to live with the thoughts that Vinnie was not immortal and was subject to illness and injuries. When they ate out with Vinnie's friends and family Mark had to indulge in human food for appearances sake. He constantly had to be sure to eat just enough to pass as "human" but not so much that he later became ill as his system tried to process the alien substances. When they ate with Vinnie's Italian family that process could be tricky, i.e. eating enough not to insult the cook (particularly if Vinnie's mom was the cook) but not so much Mark later spent the night retching.

Then there was the whole "acceptance" issue to deal with. While Vinnie's family, despite their strict old world Italian views, had slowly reconciled to the idea that Vinnie was gay and was now part of a gay couple (*the fact Mark was also a vampire was never mentioned to any of them, naturally*) the supernatural world still looked down on such "mixed" relationships. On those occasions when Mark was forced to go to some social event in the community, the snubs directed toward Vinnie were never subtle. Of course, the time Vinnie punched out a rather overtly threatening drunken ogre did raise him up a bit in the estimation of some, but still Mark, with Jaime as backup, always made sure that Vinnie was never alone at these events just in case someone got the idea his human partner would make a nice aperitif. But regardless of the hassles, the two had stuck to it. They had overcome the usual and unusual roadblocks and by now they were a true devoted couple. More importantly, for the first time in decades, Mark had a place that truly felt like a home.

"So your mom came to see me today at my office," Mark said softly as he sank back into Vinnie's arms and continued speaking, enjoying the rough scraping of Vinnie's five o'clock shadow along his own shoulder's skin. "She and her friend asked me to undertake a case for them," he sighed contentedly as he nuzzled snugly further into Vinnie's spooning embrace. At over six feet and one inch, Vinnie's bulkier muscled form almost encircled Mark's own leaner, yet toned, smaller five foot nine inch frame. Mark reveled at how the touch of his taller lover's brawny physique around his still thrilled him beyond anything he had ever experienced with any other man.

"Really, my mom came to see you" Vinnie lightly replied as he pressed up against Mark and kissed the lower lobe of Mark's right ear while massaging his erection along the crack of Mark's rump. "About you helping them on a case, huh?" He asked weakly.

Mark smiled, knowing from the tenor of Vinnie's voice that her visit to him was not something that took Vinnie by surprise. He also knew that Vinnie's current bed actions were a classic maneuver he always used to dodge any serious "bed-talk" and were now particularly designed to "interrupt" the subject Mark had just brought up for discussion. "Yes, really," Mark chuckled as he rolled around to face Vinnie whose features took on a sheepish appearance of discomfort. "I knew it," Mark stated sharply. "You sent her to me didn't you?" He asked, enjoying how Vinnie was squirming under his stare. *Damn, he is so sexy when he's embarrassed about something*," Mark pondered. He tried to give his lover a stern look but found himself grinning inspite of his resolve not too do so.

Vinnie's handsome face broke out into a smile. "Aw Mark, come on I was stuck," he murmured as he pressed himself closer to Mark, letting the latter feel the hardness of his arousal.

"No you don't," Mark laughed as he pushed back a bit from Vinnie while still keeping embraced in the powerful arms of the man he loved. "I want an explanation from you, lover, or it's the couch tonight for one of us."

Vinnie blushed. "I had to send her to you," he responded, faking a pitiful demeanor. "Mom and Mrs. Castillo came into the squad room and insisted I investigate the possible homicide of Mrs. Castillo's dog." Vinnie pulled Mark tighter, engulfing the smaller vampire in his powerful grip as he began gently rubbing their crotches. "I had to do something, honey – it was embarrassing. I mean all the guys in the room were about to laugh out loud at them. I couldn't let that happen to my mom and I couldn't just open a homicide file, Mark, let alone officially investigate a dog's murder." As he finished speaking he sensually ground his hips further into Mark's. By now Vinnie's manhood was at full staff. "Don't be mad," he said hoarsely as his brown eyes took on that softer unfocused look which always came to them whenever Vinnie was in sexual heat. His breathing increased and his hip movements below quickened.

Mark's own manhood also completely rose in response to the pleasurable frottage, but he was determined to finish their conversation despite his own growing state of arousal. "Why send them to me?" He asked insistently. "I mean, it's a sad situation but a dog's death, which by the way they both insist on describing as a *homicide,* is hardly something I do as a private investigator. Not to mention they are humans, which is totally outside of my normal clientele base!"

Vinnie stopped his activities and pulled back his head so Mark could fully see his face. Vinnie's eyes lost that prior dilated appearance as he focused on his lover. "It's my mom, Mark. She wanted help. How could I just blow her off? I thought sending her to you, I mean," he paused for second. "I thought it would be okay to send someone I love who needed help to someone I love to get it."

Mark stared at Vinnie seeing the total sincerity in his eyes. Vinnie was devoted to his mother and in sending her to Mark he was, after all, in some roundabout way demonstrating the intensity of his love for Mark by placing her into Mark's care. Mark smiled as he reached toward Vinnie's head to affectionately tousle the latter's curling dark hair. "It's okay, I've already begun checking around but no promises. I don't even want to think about what I'll do if I find out who did it. I mean, can they be criminally charged?"

"Oh yes they can," Vinnie answered quickly, happy Mark was going to do it and, on some level, also relieved that Mark's investigation would take him off the hook with his mom for his own failure to officially open a case. "The animal cruelty laws in this state are pretty severe. Whoever it is that did this could get jail or a heavy fine. Then there is the civil case. I bet the jury would make him pay through the nose once they see Mrs. Castillo on the stand." He said enthusiastically as he warmed to the subject.

Mark smirked as he pulled Vinnie closer to give him a light kiss across his mouth so as to terminate the discussion. "I should charge you for this case," he continued saying as he gave Vinnie a longer and more intense kiss. "Got any ideas how you might pay me, mister big time New York City homicide detective?" He chuckled as he nuzzled Vinnie's ear, playfully nipping at it. He lightly tweaked one of his lover's nipples knowing that this action particularly aroused Vinnie. As expected, the man's round orb hardened under the physical assault.

"Yes. Aw, gees Mark you know I love it when you do that to them," Vinnie grunted as his lover moved his hand over to touch the other one on his bedmate's chest. The New York City detective smiled then leaned his own head downward to kiss the soft skin of Mark's neck area. "Maybe we could work out the fee right now?" Vinnie answered huskily as he lowered his head and began kissing farther downward. His hand reached out to gently grip Mark's erection. "Maybe we can begin the first installment right now," Vinnie grunted eagerly as he expertly stroked Mark's manhood.

"By the way, did you know your mom thinks we are going to get married soon, and by your cousin the priest no less!" Mark muttered as Vinnie continued his actions. The sensation of the fingertips of his lover's other hand running down his spinal column caused him to shiver with desire. "Aw fuck yes," Mark hissed before adding, "we need…oh sweet Hera… to talk about…that." Mark moaned in delight as Vinnie began to awaken every erogenous zone in Mark's body.

"Yeah," Vinnie mumbled as his lips were otherwise occupied. "Later… talk later," he grunted as he turned Mark around. "Thanks for …my mom…your…help," he finished saying before his voice slipped into incoherent noises.

"No problem," Mark sighed in reply. "Besides, the thing isn't going to be a hassle," he groaned just before he felt Vinnie enter into him and beginning slowly thrusting. Vinnie's hand came around Mark's side and continued massaging Mark's erection. Mark shoulder felt the rough cheek of his lover gently rubbing upon it. The tingling it caused him only added to his erotic stimulations. In a few minutes Mark slipped into his own state of complete mindless arousal. Later he would recall that last statement he had made and wonder how he could have been so utterly wrong.

The next morning as the two men were dressing for work Mark decided to bring up the major subject that had not been addressed during the night. "Vinnie," he said hesitantly as he watched his lover standing in front of the bedroom mirror adjusting the tie. "You didn't…I mean, this getting married soon nonsense was just your mother's silly idea not yours, right!"

Vinnie stopped and turned toward Mark. "No, I didn't know about it," he replied in a low tone. "It was…is…all her own idea…but…**nonsense**… **silly**…the thought of you and me," he stopped talking and Mark found the air had become chilled.

At that exact moment he knew he had totally screwed up in bringing this matter up, yet the idea of an immediate marriage, or just a marriage to Vinnie, was something he'd never seriously thought about. "Look Vinnie," he quickly said as he approached his lover. "I love you completely."

"But not enough to consider ever marrying me, right!" Vinnie responded in annoyance.

"Vinnie," Mark answered, desperate not to ruin what they had. "How can we marry? I mean, I'm immortal and you…" he halted once more, realizing from the hurt in Vinnie's dark brown eyes that he had truly messed this discussion up now. "No, what I mean is…well you…" he hurried to say, trying to quickly salvage the situation.

"Yeah Mark, I know exactly what you mean," Vinnie growled as he grabbed his jacket, "Its fine. I'm merely the guy you are currently screwing for a few years till I get too old to interest you anymore, then you just turn me in like some clunker for a newer model! Or maybe you just want to be free to cut out when I get so old and infirmed I need help getting around." He yelled in frustration as he strode toward the door.

"Vinnie, that's not what I meant," Mark stated as Vinnie stormed out slamming the door behind him and leaving Mark alone in their home as a piece of him wondered if perhaps the last part of what Vinnie said was somehow true.

A Boner Book

INVESTIGATIONS AND CONFRONTATIONS

Mark was in a foul mood when he got to work. As he opened his office's front door he was greeted by the soft strains of Helen Forrest singing the lyrics to *"I'm Always Chasing Rainbows."* Somehow, he thought, Jaime just had an uncanny instinct of knowing what the hell was going on with him. There were days when Mark felt as if he was in some weird late forty's noir film, with Jaime picking just the right background score to enhance the viewer's pleasurable experience. He pushed the door open to see the local young UPS guy holding Jaime, still in a feminine form, the PI observed, locked close to him in a tight embrace while furiously kissing and groping up her leg with his other free hand.

"Ahem," Mark coughed. "I know your company provides good service but this type of customer satisfaction is a bit much, don't you think?" Mark said, finding the sight of the well built and good looking deliveryman intertwined with the smaller and slighter feminine sex demon to be interestingly both amusing, yet also somehow highly erotically stimulating. "Jaime, enough," Mark sternly said as he realized, from his own physical reactions, that his secretary was using her sex demon allure to "feed off" the sexual energy the clearly aroused deliveryman was giving off.

"Oh sure thing, boss," Jaime replied, opening her eyes. "We didn't see you, did we Simon," she said with a girlish giggle that was utterly entrancing. The young UPS man was clearly, however, still oblivious to the vampire's presence. By now he was busy kissing Jaime's neck while reaching upward to grab an anatomical part of Jaime's upper body. This was something Mark was not prepared to witness.

"Jaime," Mark hissed. "Turn it all the way off and lets get back to work right now!"

Jaime sighed her reluctant agreement, then easily pushed Simon away. "Another time, hot stuff," Jaime cooed as she lightly kissed the young man and moved out from under his grasp. The dazed and rather obviously stimulated Simon stood before them blinking and shaking his head as the "allure effect" slowly eased out of his system. Jaime smiled and adjusted her sheer flower patterned dress. "By the way, you like, boss?" She quizzed girlishly as she twirled in the dress, showing off her attire so as to give Simon time to cool off. "A high-waisted gore skirt with ruching on the upper sleeves and lower skirt. I think these puffed sleeves are so…" Jaime laughed as she watched a flush of embarrassment come across Simon's handsome face as he came to full realization that he was still sporting a rather impressive tent-pole in his uniform's pants in front both of them.

"Uh…I…gotta go Mr. Julian," the young man said as he picked up his sign-in board off the desk and scurried out in a panic.

Mark shook his head. "I swear Jaime, sometimes you really push it."

"Mark please, first my alarm failed to go off so I woke up late. I skipped my breakfast. A girl's got to eat, you know." Jaime answered with an exaggerated pout.

"Not today, Jaime." Mark groused as he walked past her into his private office. "Just not in the mood today."

Jaime followed him in. "Okay, what did you two boys fight about? "She inquired sympathetically.

"Who said Vinnie and I fought," Mark shot back weakly.

Jaime rolled her eyes. "Oh please, it's THAT clear boss. Now shoot me the story."

Although Mark had not intended to say anything he found himself telling Jaime everything that had happened. When he finished he glanced up at Jaime, "Okay, how bad. Go on, tell me I fucked up royally."

Jaime nodded, "boss, you just told yourself that very thing." She saw the pain in Mark's face. "Don't worry, it will blow over. Dear Goddess you two are so much in love even I get a jolt whenever you are together."

Mark's eyes widened in horror as a humiliating thought raced across his brain, "Jaime, you don't ever…feed off us do you?" He quizzed in embarrassment over such a concept.

"OH PLEASE," Jaime loudly replied as Mark blushed at having even brought the issue up. "Don't you two wish," she answered as she returned to her desk while watching as Mark sighed with relief. She suppressed a small devilish grin while thinking, *"maybe a short sip now and then when I need a small sexy warm jolt of something in place of a cup of hot Joe!"*

"By the way," Mark called out from his desk as he reviewed his papers. "What's with the UPS guy? I thought you were coupled up with that sexy Latino doorman who works over at the gay bar in the Upper East Side?"

"Ah dear," sighed Jaime, "I kind of wore him out. We broke up before he had a stroke during sex. I need a guy who is more va…va…va boom in bed, boss!"

Mark shook his head and laughed. "I got it. Hey Jaime, do we have any vet's death or police report or something which describes how Mrs. Castillo's Lab was killed?" He inquired as he searched the assembled information and typed notes on Mrs. Castillo's case.

"I'm not sure they do official police reports but I thought you might want something, so I checked with our client. There was an official lost dog complaint filled with the police. Her son claimed the dog's body and he saw the animal at the vet before it was cremated. I'm going to see him this morning to get a statement before he flies back to his camp in San Diego," Jaime stated.

"Great. Go right now then," Mark said. "Oh and Jaime, just nail me that report and not the Marine, got it?"

"Why boss," Jaime laughed as she opened her compact and fixed her makeup, "I know how to act." She applied her lipstick and sauntered happily out the door, leaving a bemused Mark pondering if, like the Marines, Jaime was just an ordinary sex demon seeking "a few good men."

PRECINCT DETOURS

Vinnie was engrossed in reading his case files when he noticed the usual bedlam of the squad room had gone silent. Then he heard a few guys whistle. When he looked up he saw a smiling Jaime striding toward him with a confidence borne out of an inner knowledge that all eyes were now firmly riveted on her. By the slight tingling in his crotch he knew that the stunningly attractive sex demon was emanating her allure for the crowd. Thankfully it was on a low voltage but if Vinnie, who was now completely gay, could feel this stimulation from a womanly form then the other heterosexual detectives and uniformed officers must be really feeling it. When he glanced around he saw quite a few of the younger uniformed cops were quickly grabbing files to hold in front of their crotches. "Gees Jaime," Vinnie said with a smile as Jaime sat down next to him while nodding a grin to the other red-faced men in the room. "The guys here gotta lot of work to do today so can you turn… you know… your *specialty* into the "off mode" for just awhile?"

Jaime smirked and nodded. Vinnie suddenly sensed a subtle change in Jaime's demeanor along with a drop in his own sexual "itchiness." The squad's noise levels rose as the other men in the room tried to appear busy or, in some cases, attempted to get out of the place without revealing their semi-arousals.

"So why the visit, hot stuff?" Vinnie asked, amused by the display he was observing in his usually unflappable hardnosed coworkers.

"I came for a dead dog's police report and detoured up here to see you on the side. We need to talk in private, sexy," Jaime answered.

"Follow me, then," Vinnie responded as he got up from his desk chair and led Jaime to a nearby interview room. Just before they entered it Jaime reached down to goose the hot looking detective's hard rounded rump in front of the whole squad room.

"What the hell was that for?" A shocked Vinnie asked as he closed the door behind them.

"Just giving you some street credit in front of your peers who, if they know you are gay, should also know you are still one hell of a sexy Italian dude." Jaime sighed in girlish innocence. "Now this is about Mark's current difficulties."

"Is he alright?" Vinnie asked with concern. "He's not in any danger is he?" He quizzed the sex demon as suddenly thoughts of their previous blowup vanished from his mind.

"Ah, I knew you still loved him," Jaime laughed.

"For the love of God, you fucking scared me!" Vinnie said as he ran his fingers through his dark curls in relief. "Look Jaime, this really isn't something I want to talk about."

"Good because I want you to just listen, got it you gorgeous man," Jaime replied as she sat down and crossed her legs, giving Vinnie a nice look at her well-formed(to use a forties term that Jaime would appreciate) gams and trim figure. "Mark is so crazy in love with you it scares him."

"Well, it scares me, too," Vinnie started to state before Jaime signaled him to keep still.

"As I said, sweetie, my boss is nuts over you," Jaime continued. "He is so crazy in love over you he is scared stiff."

Vinnie was about to break in but then saw Jaime shoot him a firm look not to interrupt again.

"Honey, you love a vampire and that, my dear, is a big deal. Not for the usual reasons, mind you, but…" Jaime sighed, pondering how to say this just right. "Okay, you have got to try to visualize it as he sees it. Right now you are going to be thirty-two years old but you honestly look like you are still in your late twenties. Mark died at twenty-two but looks a few years older." Jaime saw Vinnie's raised eyebrow at that last observation. "Please, those old Romans had a tough life. It's a wonder they ever got past their thirties. Of course that ages you a tad more in appearances. But this is beside the point," Jaime insisted before she continued. "You are aging and he isn't. In ten years, no matter how you slice the beef, he will still look amazingly young. How is THAT going to be explained to your family, or your friends? What does he do in the face of this situation? Does he disappear to spare you those silly unbelievable explanations you will have to cook up? This is also assuming you could ever successfully lie to your mother, which frankly, having met that lovely woman, I truly doubt you are capable of doing AT ALL!" Jaime paused, watching as the full ramifications of this idea played out in Vinnie's mind. Satisfied she was doing fine, she took a deep breath and went forward in her lecture. "Or another alternative then. Does he go into hiding or become some hermit and only hole up with you while skipping all your future family and/or work events? How will that one play out? Lastly dear, there is the issue that really strikes home: he has to watch you become ill and then eventually die."

Vinnie's face registered the thought of that last statement with all its implications. He shuddered. "Should we…" Vinnie stayed silent for a few minutes, then hesitantly he continued. "Are you saying we should end it now? I can't do that, Jaime. I can't leave him ever!"

Jaime smiled. "Good boy. I knew that was true. I'm just saying give him room. Unless you are willing to convert, there is an eight hundred pound gorilla in the room you two have to acknowledge. So he's skittish about the future. He tries not to see what is ahead for you both. Cut him some slack, you handsome idiot."

"Convert?" Vinnie asked in confusion. "From Roman Catholic to what, a pagan like him or?"

Jaime grew serious." I mean convert as in…" Her voice trailed off.

"Vampire…me?" Vinnie finished the unspoken meaning. "Gees… wow…I mean…I never even considered," he muttered as he contemplated such a life and his place in it.

"Another time and another man for that particular discussion, baby," Jaime retorted lightly. "Now I had to miss lunch to accomplish this nice chat we just had, so if you will be so kind as to wait here for a few minutes while I leave through the squad room."

"Why?" Vinnie quizzed then stopped as the light of knowledge dawned on him. "Feeding, huh?"

"Yes, darling," Jaime chuckled as she rose and adjusted her form fitting sheer dress that, in the right overhead light, left nothing to the imagination. "This girl really needs to feed off some hot cop sex vibes, so I'm waltzing out there using fifty percent allure power." She reached for the door handle and turned to Vinnie. "Later now, dear! Oh by the way, I'm running another errand involving a hot sexy Marine who is off on a long flight and might like something to think about while he's flying. Mark is stuck in the office. I will be gone for quite a long time," Jaime innocently coughed then winked knowingly. With that, Jaime turned and walked out.

Vinnie waited a few moments, spending the time thinking over everything Jaime had said. He left the room, noticing as he did so that quite few detectives had loosened their collars and, even more amusing, several young, good looking uniformed officers were trying to subtly adjust obvious mounds in their crotches. "Jaime," he softly chuckled as he grabbed his jacket off his chair and left the squad room to find Mark in order to passionately grab him to engage in mad monkey sex. As Vinnie hit the streets he also pondered whether his sudden overwhelming urge to get extremely physical with the man he loved might not be due to a parting "gift" from the sex demon. "Who the hell cares anyway," he said out loud as he hailed a cab to get to Mark's office faster! When he arrived he found Mark seated at his desk, reading reports. Mark looked up but before he could say a word Vinnie had come up beside him, pulled him from his chair, proceeded to kiss Mark hard and deep and then, amid a tumbling of papers, had his heated way with a thoroughly shocked but extremely agreeable Mark right there on the PI's desk! Lost in an afterglow they never heard the outer door open or someone enter until they heard him speak.

"I believe the current correct modern expression is to say, when one sees others engaged in such a situation, **get a room,** but technically you are in a room so on some level I doubt those words accurately fit. But really, gentlemen, to find you both in *flagrante delicto* during working hours!" The cultured, lightly Spanish accented voice said as Tortego, accompanied by another rather obviously well built six foot two young blonde vampire, watched the two mortified and completely naked men scramble to re-dress with some small shred of dignity. As they clumsily scooped up their clothes Tortego casually smirked at them. His companion, who clearly had to be a vampire as well if he was with Tortego, merely gazed at them both with his icy blue eyes. Though he did not speak, his look indicated that he felt polluted being near them. Unlike Tortego, who though severe in his choice of dress was always fashionable in a designer suit and tie, this vampire wore simply a pair of nondescript black pants combined with a black long sleeved turtleneck sweater.

ANOTHER REQUEST NOT TO BE DENIED

"I have a matter that you must handle for me, Marcus Claudius Marcellus," the bemused vampire leader sighed as he finally sat in a chair. He signaled to his companion to wait outside in the outer room. The solemn young man, who had yet to utter a word since his arrival, nodded and silently left them. "Oh that is Jorgen, my personal bodyguard who also serves as the head of my security team," Tortego said nonchalantly, as if the information was of no importance. "Just in case you are wondering about him. I need one at present with me at all times now for reasons which compel this visit."

As Mark and Vinnie dressed Tortego waited, cradling his chin on his fingertips. "You can stay too, human, as well," he said as Vinnie pulled up his pants. "It might involve your community on some small level. As if," Tortego snorted with distain, "I should truly care about that contingency in light of the current potentially critical situation we are faced with!" He pursed his lips with annoyance as Mark fumbled with the buttons of his shirt. "Are you ready yet, Marcus Claudius Marcellus, or do you need more time to gather your senses."

"I'm always ready, Tortego," Mark, now completely dressed, retorted sharply as he sat onto his chair while Vinnie stood behind him. "Oh, the name is Mark, okay. I think you know this fact so try not to screw it up when you address me after this. Last time, I'm called Mark Julian now, got it!"

"Ah yes, Julian," Tortego sneered, "an amusing variation on your dead wife's last name as I recall, isn't it." He glanced up at Vinnie, "You do know Marcus, excuse me Mark, was once married to a woman. History says she was a bit of tart, as I recall too."

Mark tensed, ready to reach out and grab the haughty ascetic looking vampire across from him and haul him over the desk so he could beat the hell out of him. "History, as I recall," Mark said with barely controlled rage, "says you and your buddies on the Inquisition were a bunch of sadistic closet queens. I think though they got it wrong regarding my late wife – they nailed you dead on!"

Tortego's dark eyes grew even darker. The beginnings of fangs appeared inside the old Spaniard's mouth. Mark felt himself calling up his vampire persona in response when suddenly he felt Vinnie's hand squeezing his shoulder. Quickly he regained control. Tortego observed the change in Mark and he too drew back.

"Mark doesn't keep secrets from me, Mr. Tortego," Vinnie said, breaking in to cool off the atmosphere in the room. "But you said you came here to ask for Mark's help in some matter so we should not waste your time trading in old gossip."

Tortego straightened in his chair and glared at Vinnie. "I did not 'ask' him for anything, human. I believe I said I had an assignment for him," he hissed.

"It all rather boils down to a question of semantics, don't you think? You need his help. Why split hairs," Vinnie calmly replied, as Mark silently enjoyed watching his lover take on the former Inquisitor.

"In my days on the Inquisition the question of semantics was always critical, human," Tortego replied swiftly.

"And look how good that all turned out for your crew," Vinnie retorted calmly as a grin came to Mark's face.

"ENOUGH WORD PLAY!" Tortego unexpectedly yelled, clearly annoyed to be in the midst of this verbal joust with a human.

Mark had to confess, inwardly he wondered why Tortego had just reacted to such an extent by the verbal dueling. He assumed now that Tortego must be under some type of a tremendous stress to let his discomfort show to Mark and especially to Vinnie.

The vampire leader seemed to take cognizance of his overreaction, as well. He paused, then slowly resumed speaking, using an even tone of voice. "The matter I am here upon is critical and time is of the essence for its solution."

"I'm, or rather, we, are listening," Mark said firmly.

Tortego shifted in his chair. "I need you to find a certain animal."

"*Another fucking animal case*," Mark thought in anger. "*What the hell is going on?*" He controlled his desire to scream and simply asked, "any particular kind of animal?"

Tortego grinned, "a very particular one, Mark Julian. I need you to find out who kidnapped that arrogant young werewolf who goes by the name of Jean-Claude Roué!"

Mark blinked. Although he had never met the young man, his reputation as a rebel on the council was the prime topic for the supernatural community gossips. Everyone knew how much he battled for his clan and of his clashes with Tortego's leadership style and power. If Tortego wanted him found Mark wanted to know the reason he did so. "Why do you care?"

Tortego took a deep breath, "it seems Jean-Claude vanished right after the last council meeting. That gathering ended with some ill considered words by myself which," he paused as he considered his next words, "might have given some people the outlandish idea that I wished harm toward him."

"Did you?" Vinnie quizzed, as he went into his cop interrogator mode.

Tortego grimaced. Mark knew the arrogant vampire probably hated being subjected to questioning about his desires, especially by a human, but so far he had resisted the urge to get up and leave. Things were decidedly interesting.

"I bear no one any malice, nor have I ever felt it in the past toward anyone, nor shown it to others," Tortego insisted. Seeing both of the other two men give him a look of utter disbelief Tortego merely sighed with resignation and continued. "I may have, on occasion, demonstrated by my demeanor something that could be seen to appear to contradict what I just stated but that is not the issue at hand. His clan thinks I am involved in Jean-Claude's vanishing. When they returned from their country estate and found him gone they made inquiries. Naturally, my enemies pointed the finger of blame at me, or a vampire who was acting under my orders. They have given me to the next full moon to produce their "crown prince" safe and unharmed or…"

"It descends into an all out war between their kind and ours," Mark said. "The end result of which is for one side to be eliminated, leaving the other group to pick up the pieces. Of course, that depends on if, one assumes, the victorious side is in any shape to do it, right?"

"Yes," Tortego admitted. "Even if we won we'd be so depleted in our ranks we would be easy prey for those other supernatural factions that would merely sit the conflict out and wait like vultures to swoop in later for the prize. In any event I feel that such a war would not be advantageous for our people at this time. So, will you find him for us before that next full moon cycle?"

"*Not advantageous for you because you might lose the war or lose your sole authority in any future peace treaty,*" Mark decided. Mark hated the vampire leader and was loath to aid him in any manner. In his view, Tortego's rigid refusals to share power had brought this situation about. The vampire kingpin had his own minions, Mark decided. Let them handle it.

"Why not use Jorgen out there and his team?" Mark asked, noticing that the blonde security vampire stiffened when he heard this statement. No doubt, Mark figured, the guy felt the same way about the matter.

"I need some looking who is," Tortego coughed then smiled, "not so closely connected with me. To assure some in our group I am serious about the mission. You have a sterling reputation for being independent of factions, and with regard to your well-known views about myself that…well, let me just say I feel it is more politically advantageous to use your services right now for this delicate set of circumstances."

Mark was about to refuse the request when Vinnie unexpectedly spoke out. "We will happily be of assistance, Mr. Tortego, and thank you for your trust in our ability to render you aid in this matter. Right, Mark?"

Tortego, and even Mark, were rendered speechless by Vinnie's words, albeit for different reasons.

"Thank you," Tortego said as he rose from his chair, delighted by Vinnie's quick agreement and the respectful way Vinnie had addressed him. The former Spanish inquisitor had expected to end up arguing for Mark's aid. "Well, I will go so you can begin," Tortego quickly said as he pulled a thick envelope out from his jacket's inside pocket. "Here is a full report of everything we know about it. Gentlemen, if you will now excuse me, I have pressing critical council business to handle so…" with that he rose. "Oh," he said as he turned to leave. "Normally full moons happen every thirty days or so. You are aware this particular month is somewhat unusual in that the moon will be full at two distinctly separate times during one thirty day period. I believe humans refer to this second lunar event as a blue moon. I rather like the poetic quality of this reference. Now, unfortunately more than a few days have passed since we first learned about Jean-Claude's disappearance so I'm afraid that gives you, I'd imagine, just ten days at best to find him. Well, business calls," he concluded as he rapidly exited the offices accompanied closely by a grim faced Jorgen.

"That lousy bastard waited till the last second to tell us that choice bit of news," Mark grumbled. He turned his head to look up at Vinnie.

"Cute bodyguard, if you are into that whole scary but muscular and hot Germanic, Aryan, Nordic type, huh," Vinnie chuckled, hoping to ease the upcoming potential storm he observed in Mark's visage with a dose of humor.

"Why did you say we'd help that son-of-a-bitch," Mark heatedly asked. "Like we'd care if he lost his position or got snuffed during some stupid turf war?"

"I don't give a damn about him," Vinnie replied forcefully. "If that bastard was staked out in the sun I'd sell tickets. Hell, I might even pour honey on his wounds and toss on a few cups of fire ants to really make it a fun day."

"Then why did you agree that we'd help him, honey?" Mark repeated as he got off his chair to face Vinnie.

Vinnie smiled when he heard Mark use that reference term toward him. He knew then they were back in sync. "Because, lover," he answered as he reached out to stroke Mark's cheek. "A war between werewolves and vampires has two major concerns for me. One officially and one not so official."

"Which are?" Mark continued as he enjoyed the touch of the only man he truly ever fully loved gently stroking his cheek with his strong fingers.

He was happy as well that their argument had been smoothed over, at least for now.

"Well, the fact that officially there would be at least the potential of collateral human injury or deaths if any humans happened to be in the wrong place at the wrong time when battles take place."

"And the unofficial one," Mark said as he pulled Vinnie close toward him. He riveted his eyes onto Vinnie's and felt the warmth of his lover's powerful body on his own slightly smaller one. Slowly, his vampire's highly developed sense of smell took in the heady perfume of Vinnie's own unique human scent.

"It seems that I am going steady with a vampire who might be attacked by some big bad wolf just because he is a vampire," Vinnie stated as he leaned in to deeply kiss Mark before pulling back to say, "I don't like my boyfriend hurt or subject to even the slightest of discomforts. Unless the latter is a byproduct of playing with me during our more friskier endeavors." He chuckled as he touched the bridge of Mark's nose with one of his fingertips then followed it with another passionate kiss. "Oh, and for the record, regarding the buff blonde boy before," Vinnie added, "he is not my type at all. I am totally fixated on shorter Roman men, especially one in particular."

Mark grinned during their kiss. "I know," he murmured. "By the way, you made points with Tortego by agreeing and being so respectful about it when you did agree we would help him." Mark interjected between their kisses. "You really know how to suck up and kiss ass, huh, toward the big boys when it matters."

"Well, I never had any complaints about my ass kissing ability," Vinnie grunted in pleasure as he felt the both of them physically heating up. "I kiss great ass. Let me show you how great." He growled as he turned Mark around while loosing the PI's belt. "Yeah, I do it just fine in that regard don't I?" He finished saying as he pulled Mark's pants down and bent the aroused PI face forward over his own desk. Rapidly Vinnie dropped his own suit pants and fell to his knees behind Mark, holding the latter's hips with his hands for support as Vinnie moved his face forward, adding as he began, "well, don't I do it just fine lover?"

"Oh Jupiter Best and Greatest, that you do Vinnie," Mark whimpered as round two of what had been interrupted by Tortego commenced.

Two hours later the men re-dressed for the second time. In fact they had just picked up Mark's scattered papers from the floor and arranged the desk when a giddy Jaime sailed into the outer office humming the United States Marine Corp's battle hymn.

"I think Jaime just did Mrs. Castillo's baby boy!" Mark sighed as a smiling Jaime marched into the inner office.

"Well, he was going to board a plane when I caught up with him, and you know how strict security is nowadays on the issue of carrying loaded weapons and all." Jaime said as she recalled her airport encounter with the strikingly good-looking and extremely buff young Marine.

"There is a point to that statement," Vinnie asked as he shook his head trying not to picture Jaime and someone he knew from the neighborhood doing what he could only imagine was done.

Jaime smirked. "I did my part for security by helping my Marine make sure ALL his weapons were properly and totally discharged before he boarded his flight back to his base. Good thing it's a long flight too because that boy was moving funny when he walked toward the departure gate."

"Oh God, please let me run a faucet over my brain to wash out what I just visualized," Vinnie chuckled as he contemplated how homophobic and super macho Charles might react of he knew he had gotten it on with a girl who was also, at times, a guy!

"Well honestly, fellas," Jaime responded, affecting an innocent look. "I missed lunch AGAIN thanks to Mark's assignments. I have to eat don't I? Besides," she paused and looked around the room, then closed her eyes for a second, "my sex demon senses seems to detect…" she stopped speaking and smirked at Mark and Vinnie who both blushed and looked away. "Ah, a bit of heavy lifting here, huh guys."

"Okay, let's get down to business," Mark coughed, anxious to change the subject.

"Sure thing, guys," Jaime chuckled. "But my senses tell me you two did get down on some pretty heavy business already."

"Gees Jaime," a blushing Vinnie wailed. "Give us a break!"

"Okay I'll stop," Jaime sighed in disappointment. "By the way, as I was coming in here I saw Mr. Tortego walking through our lobby with a pretty smoking hot blonde vampire type on his heels." Jaime prattled. "Not too shabby in the hard-body department, I'll tell you guys. The blonde and I actually physically bumped into each other. Purely accidentally, I swear," she said as the other two men shot her a look showing they did not believe that statement for one second. "Okay," Jaime groused, knowing that even she couldn't hope to be believable on this point. "Maybe I kind of got in his way as the Nordic God raced along after Mr. Happy. Anyway, he at least helped me up onto my feet after we fell. I admit I kind of brushed up close to him as we were sprawled on the floor, but to be fair, when he got me on my feet he pulled me toward him to, you know, steady me on my feet. I did take advantage to lean into him for a quick "check of the goods" but I promise blonde boy liked it. He even smiled and took an extra second to brush up harder against me, as well, before he raced to join Tortego in their limo. A bit severe in his dress but his choices in jewelry were rather interesting," Jaime stated as she recalled how she had admired the unusually designed ring she saw when his strong hand reached down to pull her to her feet. "So what's up with the visit from Mr. No Personality?"

A Boner Book

HAPPENINGS IN THREE PLACES AT THE SAME TIME

In The Office

Mark looked at Vinnie to display an attitude of mock annoyance. "It seems our office has been hired by Tortego to find a missing council member, thanks to my boyfriend over here."

Vinnie smirked in amusement as he leaned his tall well-built frame against the nearby wall. "Well, you gotta pay rent and a money case is a money case, right?" He replied.

Jaime gazed at the two now smiling men and knew their differences, for now, had been either resolved or put off for the present. "Okay boss, what is the case, or rather, who is the missing council member?" She inquired eagerly.

Mark stopped smiling as he recalled Tortego's visit. "Jean-Claude Roué has been kidnapped and Tortego wants us to find him fast!"

"Goddess' blood!" A surprisingly shocked and shaken Jaime said before quickly composing herself. "Mark, that's really big time." She went on, trying to appear nonchalant about what she had just heard while attempting to cover up her initial reaction to the news. "I mean Jean-Claude ranks right up there in the supernatural community. He's even famous among humans here as an incredibly rich, good-looking young man about town who does a lot of charity and dates supermodels. Mark, you have to find him." Jaime said, a touch too much vehemence in her voice.

Vinnie and Mark looked at the young sex demon. The formers cop's instinct and Mark's vampire senses observed something in her overall demeanor that both simultaneously thought bore further inquiry. "Jaime, is there something you need to mention about this matter or about Jean-Claude in particular?" Mark asked.

Jaime stood before them in silence for a few minutes, then softly answered. "Guys it wasn't easy growing up as a half-breed in our community. Having a sex demon for one parent and a shape shifter for another…well, a lot of kids in the supernatural world here shunned me. I wasn't invited to many parties, or had any friend at all, in fact. Then one day, I must have been about thirteen or so, I received an invitation the attend Jean-Claude's sixteenth birthday party." As she spoke a far away look came over Jaime's eyes as a part of her distant past reappeared before her in her mind's eye. "I mean, it was out of the blue – a personal invitation to me to attend a party from a family who were at the pinnacle of New York City's supernatural society. Even more amazing was when I arrived there at his house. I was seated at the main table just a few chairs away from Jean-Claude. Everyone saw me. He even came over and spoke with me for twenty minutes. Then he took me out on the dance floor for a dance in front of everyone there at the party. It was like a dream. After that, no one ever snubbed me again. I mean," Jaime, continued as a huge smile came over her beautiful face, "he was THE golden boy of our society and he talked with me. If he thought I was good enough to be at his party… Well, to snub me after that would be like saying he was wrong or…no one would dare to do that and insult him or his family. Later I found out he had learned of what was being done to me. He had insisted I be invited and sit near him. Even afterwards he always made it a point to wave or say hello to me when we passed each other in our school. Guys, he made the rest of my childhood bearable." Jaime stopped as the old memories brought tears to her eyes.

"Then I'll find him," Mark replied with a husky voice. Quickly, he filled Jaime in on everything that had occurred in the office with Tortego.

"I'll take a few personal days off starting now and join you, Mark," Vinnie agreed, trying not to display too much emotion himself.

"Okay this case takes precedence." Mark said. "We skip all other cases and take no new ones on until this matter is completed."

"Even over Mrs. Castillo's I guess." Vinnie dejectedly said. logically knowing that case had to be among those being put off, too, but dismayed over how that fact would go down with his mother when she and her friend called to ask about the matter's progress.

Mark frowned. There was no question of what had to be their priority but still he remembered that crying woman's painful need for justice and, more important, how critical it was not to let Vinnie's mom feel her request for his help was unimportant for Mark. "When Mrs. Castillo calls tomorrow we can just delicately tell her…well we cannot bring up this supernatural thing and I won't lie to Vinnie's mom either…so lets just inform them both…shit, does anyone have an idea of a diplomatic way of saying…" He glanced at the other two of them for some assistance.

"Let me handle the dog case, boss. while you two concentrate on finding Jean-Claude," Jaime suddenly piped up. "After all, I set up the appointment with them. Besides, I know the file and I took Charlie's verbal statement to type up later. Why not just let me follow any clues that pop up?"

Mark and Vinnie glanced at each other. "I'm not sure about having you go solo on your first case. I mean, what if you run into trouble?" Mark replied with concern.

Jaime crossed her arms in front of her and sighed. "It's a dog, Mark. I'm not seeking out some crazy fiendish psycho murderer for the Goddess' sake. Besides," she said sweetly, "if I run into ANY trouble I'll reach out to my two big strong men okay?"

"How much trouble can this get her into, Mark?" Vinnie responded. "She'll call us, too, if she gets in over her head, which is doubtful."

Mark shook his head, "Yeah okay you are both right. Jaime, the case is yours but if you even smell a potential problem…"

"I'll call you both at once. I understand, boss." Jaime quickly agreed.

"By the way just for curiosity's sake did you get anything useful from the Marine…and I DO NOT mean what you are thinking by that statement young lady, so you can take that snide snickering smile you just got right off that face." Mark chuckled.

"Did I ever, guys," Jaime gushed before becoming serious to reflect her new professionalism. "Charles told me that his mom's Lab had been disemboweled. In fact, they found the poor creature's heart lying next to its body."

Vinnie shuddered at hearing this. He wondered about the sick mind that would do this sort of thing to some defenseless creature. Then he wondered if endorsing Jaime's handling of the case by herself might, in light of this fact, be a mistake. He was about to speak up but then decided things had gone too far to throw a monkey wrench into the idea.

"In addition," Jaime went on to report, "the dog had some type of weird symbol burned into its heart."

"What kind of symbol?" Mark queried. "Was he able to tell you what it looked like? It may be very important in finding who did this to Mrs. Castillo's dog!"

"I know, boss. Charles had trouble accurately describing it to me but he recalled exactly what it looked like, however. On the flight back to his base he is going to draw it for me then fax it here." Jaime answered, proud at what she had learned and accomplished thus far. "Charles is an artist, you know, so I'm sure the drawing will be quite good, too."

Mark sighed. "I guess that covers it for now, guys," he said, then with a fast glance at Jaime, "and girl. We have two highly important cases and a very strict time frame on at least one of them so…"

"Well, then you guys and yours truly best get a good night's sleep and tomorrow begin working on our respective cases, huh boss," Jaime sighed as she anticipated even less time in her future to eat now that she had her own case assignment. Still, the thought of solely handling her very own case for investigation was thrilling. A part of her then recalled Jean-Claude. How charming and kind he had been to her back then at his party. Even at a time when her sex demon powers had not yet developed, she had experienced the inner rush of his powerful sexuality when they had danced together. She silently prayed to the Great Goddess to keep him safe and to let Mark and Vinnie find him quickly. She then put her worries out of her mind. Time to be a detached professional. "I imagine Mr. Tortego's having to hire you went down quite well with his security chief. I'd love to have the ability to shape shift into being a fly in that limo to hear the discussion he and my blond Nordic god are probably having over this very fact right now," she chuckled.

Meanwhile in that traveling limousine.

As their armored limo drove off, carefully maneuvering through the New York City traffic, Jorgen finally spoke to his leader. "Sir, do you trust that PI and his human, whatever they are to each other, to accomplish this assignment in sufficient time to avoid a war? I mean, you saw how low he has become. Bad enough he fornicates with a human but he is doing his fornicating with a human of the same sex," he grumbled. "I'm also told he also has some half breed shape shifting sex demon as his secretary. I don't trust them or have any confidence in Mark Julian's abilities!"

Tortego smiled, debating whether to inform Jorgen that the pretty young girl he had bumped into and then smiled at was the sex demon. He shook his head knowing his chief of security had no sense of the ironic and decided not to not bring it up. "I do not endorse either of Julian's actions but I will admit he does get the job done. In that last matter he handled for the council, he and his human not only found our rogue vampire, they nicely and discreetly disposed of him for us without any extra adverse publicity."

"A total fluke I'm sure," Jorgen grunted in disgust. "But sir," Jorgen insisted, "I have a special select team of my own vampires, and as your head of security I think we could handle this situation better than those perverts."

Tortego gazed at the younger vampire, "I want Jean-Claude found safe and, even more critical, alive after he is found. While I'm sure you could, perhaps, accomplish the finding him safe part quite effectively," he said pausing to let the dig hit home. "I need to be sure when he is found he stays that way. Let me just state it out loud right now for your understanding. I think you might not hesitate to…shall we say, get rid of a thorn in my side once you had him in your grasp."

Jorgen opened his mouth to protest but was interrupted by a wave of Tortego's hand. He opened his mouth again and barely got out another, "but sir," before he was stopped once more by the now visibly mad vampire leader.

"Enough, I told you. I will not keep repeating myself or engage in an argument with you on my decision or regarding any decisions I make, now or in the future! I have decided this issue. As my old churchmen used to say, '***Rome has spoken, the subject is closed***'! I need no second guessing by any of my bodyguards, particularly from you Jorgen, on what is the proper thing to do in this matter." Tortego snarled inwardly, still angry at the verbal contest with Vinnie that had occurred in Mark's offices and, even more so, with his uncharacteristic loss of composure.

"May I respectfully then suggest we make plans to keep you in a secure place for the time being," Jorgen slowly said. "Just in case they fail in their mission and a war immediately breaks out around us. My team has secured impregnable quarters for you nearby. We can be there in five minutes."

Tortego was about to agree to that suggestion just to secure some immediate peace of mind during the limo ride, but there was something subtle yet distinctly eager in Jorgen's voice for this idea that held him back from giving his security chief permission to immediately take him to such a place right now. "*I must be imagining things because of all this stress,*" Tortego contemplated. "*He is merely anxious for my safety and annoyed at my refusal to let him and his team find that blasted werewolf.*" He gazed out the window, taking in the sights of the city. After a short pause he gave out a heavy sigh. "Not yet, although I appreciate your concern for my well being. I cannot be seen by others to be in hiding. It would have bad consequences for fear to be seen in, or suspected, with regards to myself." He turned his head to face a now clearly disappointed Jorgen. "*I will need him and his underlings if there is a war so it might be best to toss him a crumb and not risk alienating him*," he inwardly decided. "Maybe you are right. Why don't you personally keep an eye on Julian and his human friend's activities. Be discrete about it, though. Report to me with any information you come across that you feel I should know!"

A smile came over the muscled blonde vampire's face. "Yes, sir." He quickly answered, happy that he had gotten at least half of what he wanted at present. "*The idiot. The smug stupid arrogant idiot,*" Jorgen thought. "*This is what passes for leadership now. When I was a young man in Germany in the mid twentieth century, someone like him would have barely made street sweeper.*" He gazed at Tortego, "I will keep you informed about everything, sir," silently adding, *"but only those anything's I decide you need to know."* He let his thoughts drift back toward the encounter he had just had with the lithe young woman in the lobby. He felt a stirring in his crotch area. *"I must find a way to meet her again."* He mused now, contemplating his own fantasies about a possible sexual dalliance with a human. *"Sex with a human once more after so many decades. How degenerate that would be. Yes, maybe the perversion of engaging in such an activity like that can be quite stimulating after all."* He pondered as he sensed his manhood now pressing up against the tight pants he was wearing. *"If only I were alone in the car right now,"* Jorgen thought as he fought the urge to try to discreetly reach down to touch himself. He shifted subtlety in his seat, trying to adjust himself before his growing arousal was noticeable. *"Or perhaps alone in the car with that human female. Free to sexual engage at last in everything I like to do. At least with a disposable human partner I'd have none of the worries afterwards that my bed partner would talk and those in our community would hear about my rather unique erotic activity preferences."* Suddenly his sexual contemplations were rudely interrupted by Tortego's voice.

Tortego's eyes had been focused sideways once more to stare at the passing scenes outside. He shook his head. "So little time to accomplish this task and, if they fail me, an unthinkable war which could result in who knows what future consequences for our people. Let us hope they succeed, don't you agree Jorgen?" He muttered without really listening or needing any reply from his security chief.

"Yes, sir," Jorgen replied taking a deep breath and clearing his mind of his prior fantasies. "Success in one's endeavors is always very sweet. Of course, we are assuming, sir," Jorgen added with a tinge of malice, "that Jean-Claude is still alive at all!"

Tortego stiffened in his seat. He turned his head to glare angrily at Jorgen. "He lives. He lives, you understand me Jorgen!" He growled as his eyes darkened and the beginning of his fangs revealed themselves. "Any other thought is not to be contemplated," he finished saying as he calmed down, letting his features return to normal. *"But what if this is not the case? What if he was dead?*" He wondered silently with a gnawing fear inside of his very soul. "*Yes, it is best not to think such thoughts. He must still be alive,*" he decided.

"Then yes, naturally, let us hope Jean-Claude is being held alive and, in addition, being treated extremely well by whomever is currently holding him." Jorgen smirked in agreement.

Meanwhile, however, in a cage.

Jean-Claude had awakened early the next morning to find himself both naked and completely transformed back into his human form. He tried to stand but found he couldn't get his body to obey. His vision, through blurry, was clear enough for him to realize he was locked inside a cage. The cage had been built into the side wall of some type of dark windowless stone carved room whose only illuminations came from a series of lit candles set up on a nearby table. He reached out and grabbed onto the cage's bars and, through sheer force of will, he forced himself to rise to his feet. For his efforts he was immediately subjected to a series of painful stomach cramps that were so intense he began to retch. This resulted in him slipping back down onto his knees. After this latest physical reaction eased he knelt there, feeling the dampness of the large room's air chill him. "*I have to overcome all this inside me to calm my nature,*" he thought. "*I need to use my gift to its maximum advantage.*"

The young werewolf prince steadied his senses. He let his wolf nature loose to explore his surroundings by use of smells and sounds. In a few seconds he detected someone was with him in the room. As he glanced around the darkened shadows of the room he saw her form twitch. "Show yourself," he growled as another wave of nausea overpowered him, and once more he bent over and began to dry heave.

"You are only experiencing the after effects of the scorpion's toxic venom that was used to capture you, young man," a female's ragged voice croaked. "It will pass," the ancient sounding speaker giggled. "I've waited here for you to awaken," she continued saying as she moved out of the darkness into the dimmer candlelight that illuminated the dank room.

Jean-Claude took in the features of the woman. She was barely four feet tall, her yellowish white hair wildly flowed about in all directions, and her face was a mass of sagging wrinkled flesh. Her bony hands clasp each other while she grinned at him with a toothless smile. "I enjoyed watching you sleep, my young werewolf lord," she hooted in a manner that was disconcerting. Her voice carried with it an accent that was hard for Jean-Claude to place. "Such a handsome youth. Such a truly beautiful body. So defined. So nicely sleek. Filled with power. I admit I even let these old hands of mine explore your form while you slept," she hooted as her eyes took in the naked youth. "Such beauty, such a perfection of form. Such soft skin, especially in certain areas," she lewdly snickered. "It has been such a long time since my hands ran themselves along skin like that. Such nice heavy pouch and thick long equipment."

Jean-Claude experienced a mixture of disgust and rage at the thoughts of this old crone intimately touching him in his nakedness while he was helpless to resist. "Do you know, old woman?" He growled as the wolf in him raced in his blood. "Do you know the vengeance my clan will exact if I am not set free?"

"Free. Set you free you say," the old woman laughed. "No, I think not free, my beauty. No, I have plans. I have such plans, you see, for you."

"What plans?" Jean-Claude snarled as he rose upward onto to his feet. The dizziness and blurry vision seemed to be fading but the stomach cramps and the urge to vomit only intensified. Summoning all his will the young werewolf threw off the nausea. He shook at the bars. "Release me now!" He yelled with defiance.

"No," the crone wailed. "Plans, you see. Oh, plans for you," she gleefully chanted. "New full moon coming soon. A special Blue Moon. The lords of the dark arts will be gifted with you. Oh the pleasure they will have in that. The other offerings not enough. I thought the albino animal was special enough. You will be enough," she chuckled as she swayed on her feet.

"Enough for what?" The werewolf asked vehemently.

"Oh enough pleasure to give their disciple unlimited power. The touch of their divinity. Yes," the old woman said in a singsong voice. "The power of all the ancient Strega's. All the witches before. Their power given to their disciple. All just for that. The touch of the old Strega's. Just like my mother told me as a child. The ancient Stregas. Their touch. Their power. All to their disciple. All of that for offering you. I will get it…to me…the Strega's touch!"

"Offering how? In what way old woman?" Jean-Claude yelled as he futilely pulled at the cage's bars.

The ancient withered woman gazed wild-eyed at her beautiful captive wolf. "Why, when you transform you will be taken. To their altar. The beautiful boy who is also a beautiful beast. A true prince. A special gift at the special time. You will be on their altar. Then we just open you up and give them your still beating heart." She replied before beginning to rock in crazed delight." Oh, such a gift you will be for them. You will feel pain when your heart is pulled free but what is small pain when they are pleased." She began to hoot in glee. She turned to leave Jean-Claude. As she passed out of the room she blew out the surrounding candles, leaving him in total darkness.

Jean-Claude had heard the words in stunned silence. He had watched as the old woman turned to go, laughing hysterically as she did so. As he sat on the floor of his cage, shivering in the damp cold he knew three things: 1) he had find a way to escape, 2) the old woman had used the Italian word for witch: Strega which may have some relevant importance in the future toward unraveling this mystery and, 3) that old crone was completely insane!

TWO VISITS TO TWO PARKS

One park on the next day…

Jaime sat down on the grass in an area in Upper Manhattan's Highbridge Park and reviewed the police report concerning the discovery of the dog's body. Unfortunately, the report was not helpful at all. It simply set forth a set of bare boned facts that didn't even fill a quarter of the page. To be fair, Jaime assumed that finding a dead dog's killer was probably not a high priority for the vastly overworked New York City police force, which somehow kept a metropolis of over eight million souls, on the whole, safe to live out their daily lives. She re-read the notations the officer at the scene had made about the surrounding landmarks where the discovery was made, then glanced around to try and pinpoint the exact location. By her calculations, the Lab's mutilated corpse had to have been found somewhere in this very area. If she could determine the precise place where the dog's body was left maybe there might be a clue accidentally left behind by the killer. Jaime soon came to the disheartening conclusion that her search, however, was totally hopeless.

She looked out at the cliffs and massive ancient rock formations that drew so many visitors up here at Manhattan's upper reaches to spend a day just meandering about the park's open fields and wooded areas. Once this whole section of Manhattan had been solely composed of farms and estates. Now, only a few of the latter existed in this part of the city and none of the former. As she took in the pastoral scene the Highbridge Tower's' bells sounded. *"Such a peaceful place,"* Jaime thought to herself. Yet, someone around here had taken the trouble to go all the way down to Long Island to take Mrs. Castillo's dog, kill him then, dump the body here. Jaime was sure that this chosen location had to be due to the convenience of the park to the kidnapper's home. But how was she going to find the place, as well?

She got up off the grass and brushed off her well tailored "girls guide" outfit that all English scout troop leaders wore in the forties. She had bought the clothes online from a cute boutique that imported old styled English clothes to the United States. *"Not too shabby,"* Jaime pondered as she held out her compact and used it to check both the cleanliness of her garb and the straightness of the seams on her stockings. She smiled, thinking of the cost for this ensemble and how Mark would object to the fact that she had billed it to the office under "work clothes needed for undercover investigations." She let her eyes take in the sights once more and started walking toward the nearest subway entranceway. She needed to get back to the office to see if Charles had faxed her the promised illustration of the symbol he saw on the dog's heart.

"I'm starving," she mused as she strolled quietly on the forested pathway. *"No place to eat around here either and that subway ride will take at least a half hour, darn it."* As Jaime walked a young male jogger came into view. He was quite striking with curly blonde hair that clung damply to his classic Abercrombie facial features. The damp nylon blue shorts he was wearing stuck themselves suggestively to his powerful

thighs and hard tight rump. From the outline of his soggy tee shirt his upper body was nicely defined, as well. Jaime figured he was in his late twenties. As he passed her he gave her a friendly nod combined with a dazzling smile. "*Well, it is a long trip home and a girl needs her nourishment,*" she giggled to herself as she turned her head toward the retreating young man and concentrated.

A few seconds later he stopped going forward and instead just stayed where he was while continuing to jog in one place. After a few moments hesitation he abruptly turned and trotted back toward Jaime, still displaying his smile. "Hi," he said in a deeply sensual voice. "I'm Allan." He stood there giving her a quizzical look as if he couldn't figure out why he had returned.

"Hello," Jaime girlishly responded as she increase her allure almost up to its maximum potential and watched as a heated glaze of sexual arousal came over his brown eyes. Gazing downward into his crotch area Jaime observed a clearly noticeable and nicely impressive rise in the mound of his damp running shorts.

The young jogger glanced down, as well, then looked up at Jaime, blushing in a way that only increased his attractiveness. "I…please don't think," he sputtered as the sex demon sent out a powerful jolt of allure that totally silenced him by reducing him into a state of uncontrollable desire.

"I'm hungry and you obviously are working out right now, so what say we go over behind that set of bushes and do something that satisfies both our immediate objectives," Jaime stated in a matter of fact tone of voice.

Allan, by now fully in the throes of uncontainable lust, merely nodded and mumbled a hoarse "Yeah, sure thing."

Jaime took him gently by the hand and led him to a nearby out-of-the-way spot. An hour later Jaime was riding the subway back to the office, happily humming to herself while an exhausted but delightedly stunned

Allan jogged home, not only thinking that living in New York City was the greatest thing in the world, but also how was he going to explain this tryst to his boyfriend!

When Jaime returned to the office she found the eagerly anticipated fax from Charles with his expertly detailed drawing of the symbol he saw burned into the Lab's heart. As she stared at the weird design she wondered why it looked so familiar to her? Where had she seen this image before? The answered floated just out of her memory's reach. One thing she instinctively knew, however, was that it was critical she remember.

The other park...

That morning Mark and Vinnie got up very early to try and reach the park before too many tourists came through it.

"I like it when I get to go to work on a case in just jeans and a pull over," Vinnie said as he quickly grabbed his clothes out of the drawer.

"I like you in jeans," Mark chuckled as he observed how nicely Vinnie's well-developed rump looked in them. He gave Vinnie a wink, then tilted his head over towards their bed. He raised his eyebrow in a manner that clearly spoke volumes about what he had in mind.

"Work right now; hot sex later tonight," Vinnie replied with an exaggerated wink of his own as he reached over to their dresser's surface and picked up his cuffs. He twirled them suggestively before he dropped them back onto the dresser's surface.

"Yeah," Mark sighed, knowing Vinnie was right but, as always, still feeling that usual erotic heat whenever Vinnie looked that good in his clothes.

Vinnie sauntered up to Mark and took him into his arms. "How about you telling me about werewolves?" He softly asked as he leaned over to kiss Mark's ear. "Anything critical I should know, lover?"

Mark lifted his head and the two kissed. "*Yeah, thank Venus we are very okay again,*" he thought to himself. He pulled back, "No, you are right. Work now. Very hot sex later tonight." He laughed as he felt Vinnie, now hard in his jeans, brushing up closer. When Mark moved off he was happy to hear his New York City detective groan in frustration. "That will teach you to heat things up after making a strong case NOT to heat things up just now."

"Yeah," Vinnie mumbled. "Stupid. Stupid," he said as he ran his fingers through his hair, causing Mark, who knew what that action meant, to break out into more laughter.

"Werewolves." Mark began to explain to Vinnie as they ate breakfast.

"I know. I know," Vinnie sighed. "It's throw out all you believed, like the Stroker junk about vampires, right."

Mark grinned, "Actually no. In fact, the parts you hear about their changing only during full moons and silver bullet to kill stuff is spot on. I mean you can use a silver knife, too, or spear, but yes, silver is the preferred method to kill them!"

"Really?" An amazed Vinnie replied. "I thought you told me you guys encouraged misinformation among us humans to keep yourselves safe?"

"Vampires do that." Mark corrected. "Werewolves really don't seem to give a damn about that tactic. I guess if you always have to transform during a lunar cycle you pretty much can't fool people with that. If they simply keep you confined till a full moon comes up they have their proof."

"So the wild beast ripping out my heart or whatever is true as well, huh?" Vinnie grumbled, glad that a full moon was still a few days off.

The PI shook his head with amusement seeing his lover's discomfort over that possibility. "Now THAT part about the wild mindless animal is false. True, their wolf nature comes out fully but they still retain their human consciousness. Just think of them as a bigger version of a wolf whose brain thinks and acts like a humans. So if you were with them you'd just be a guy with a hell of a large pack of wolves around you. So there is no danger to someone else unless they have to defend themselves. Oh, also like Italians they are big on family and loyalty. Jean-Claude's family is very Old World in their family ties. Came over from France during the Revolution. I think you'd find them pretty much like your own relatives. Happy now, Vin?"

"Oh, ecstatic, babe," Vin grumbled.

"Besides," Mark said as he got up from the breakfast table and went over to the other side where Vinnie was sitting to tousle Vinnie's hair, "you are my significant other. Think I'd let the big bad wolf hurt that smoking body."

Vinnie stopped eating, then reached out to pull Mark down toward him. As they kissed he somehow managed to maneuver them onto the kitchen floor. "A fast one please," he moaned as he reached down to undo the pant's zipper on a now highly receptive Mark.

Mark quietly nodded as he returned the favor on Vinnie's pants. A little over an hour and a fast joint shower later they were primed for their upcoming exploration. "Okay, off to Central Park where Jean-Claude was last seen." Mark stated as the two left their domicile and walked to get the subway uptown. A rather long ride later they arrived at where they had to be.

"Do you really think we can find the place he got kidnapped, Mark?" Vinnie asked as the two of them entered entryway the northern part of New York's Central Park where Jean-Claude had last been seen. "I mean, it's a really big area we are heading into, buddy. The entire northern section is about ninety acres, give or take and acre," he joked. "Besides, it has been close to a week now since he was snatched, so as for the possibility of us finding some type of trail in the brush…well it is doubtful, Mark."

The PI turned toward his partner. "Werewolves, like most communities in the supernatural world, have a certain distinct scent. If he changed in the park, as seems likely with that last night's full moon, his wolf scent will stick around for over a week. Of course, we are assuming no other werewolves came through this area. If no one else did that then my vampire abilities should let us pick up his trail."

"Wild," Vinnie replied impressed by this fact, "by the way Mark, do I have a…you know…a distinct scent?"

Mark grinned. "Oh lover, you so do have one as well but, trust me, its an amazingly hot one!"

"Liar," Vinnie joked as the two entered further the park.

"Look, Vinnie," Mark suddenly stated as he looked around their surroundings. "Two things to keep in mind right now. One, I need you to maintain a watch for any passing park visitors for us. The scent out here in these wooded areas will be faint. That means I have to go full out into my "vampire mode" in order to enable me to concentrate solely on identifying first, then our following his smell. I won't really be aware of someone coming upon us until it is way too late. Having them see a vampire in Central Park is not a good idea right," he smirked with amusement, pondering some tourist running away screaming about blood sucking fiends and giving New York another in her numerous local urban legends. "So warn me, got it."

"Yep boss," Vinnie teased. "What is point two?"

Mark leaned in closer to Vinnie and dropped his voice. "Someone is following us. They are keeping downwind so I can't scent them, but trust me, I feel them. They may be harmless but just keep yours ears open too, buddy."

"Got it," he replied as he subtly stretched while pretending he was exploring the area within the park.

"Okay," Mark said taking a deep breath. "Here we go."

Vinnie observed as the man he loved transformed into what he also was. Mark's eyes went fully black and his fangs grew out. He seemed to be energized. A strange look came over him and for one second a chill of fear took over Vinnie's inner core of being. "*It's only the man I love. I'm totally safe*," he thought to himself, assuring the primitive instinct that all humans have in them to flee danger or the unknown.

Mark lifted his head and turned around in all directions. He first sniffed the air then by the nearby trees. His body stiffened as he took in a deep breath through closed eyes. All at once he moved along a path. He had caught Jean-Claude's faint scent. The search for where he had been going and where he had been taken was on!

For the next half hour Vinnie followed in Mark's wake as the vampire PI carefully attempted to keep to the trail the werewolf's scent leading them. They slowly walked along a path deeper into the park's Northern Woods, as that section of the park was called, until they came to the Loch Ravine and its impressive Huddlestone Arch. They went through the arch's dark tunnel, then Mark unexpectedly halted before speaking out loud. "I think …he stopped here…but…give me second…yes he must have seen the pool complex over there… he then turned around to find somewhere else to change."

Mark and Vinnie went back through the tunnel and stopped again at the other end of massive archway. Vinnie waited while Mark hunted for the werewolf scent. He had never been here before despite living all his life in New York City. He was impressed by the engineering skills of the designer who, a century and a half ago, had planned out an arch which would be constructed out of massive uncut boulders and stand ten feet high by twenty-two feet wide. It was a famous attraction for those who ventured this far north into the park because it was built without any other support to it than the force of gravity and the friction of giant rough stone upon stone. In spite of their critical mission he couldn't help but gaze around at the beauty of all this. "Got it Vinnie," he heard Mark shout as he took off onto the path toward a dense area of underbrush and trees. "I guess contemplation of nature must be for another time guys," Vinnie sighed, addressing the scenery as he left the arch to keep up with Mark. Ten minutes later Mark found what he said had to be the area where Jean-Claude was taken.

"His werewolf scent is overpowering right here," Mark said. "See, the ground covering of this place has been stomped down all around us."

"Can we follow the scent from here back to find out where he was taken?" Vinnie inquired as he used his police training to closely examine the scene.

Mark sniffed the edges of the disturbed area, then shook his head. He let his feature return to their normal state. "They used a covering agent. It's too light now to detect except right here where he was rolled up inside of whatever they carried him in to get out of here. They probably soaked it with the covering agent." He frowned. "Whoever took him was supernatural in nature. They had to know to do something like that in order to be sure they would not be followed by someone like me or his clan using their ability with scents."

Suddenly the men heard a rustling of nearby bushes. Vinnie raced toward the sound. He saw a figure and tackled it as it tried to run away. "Got you!" He yelled as the two of them rolled around in the dirt.

"Let me go, I ain't done nothing," the figure groaned as Vinnie dragged a homeless guy to his feet. "I didn't take that guy," the terrified smaller man blurted out animatedly.

"Take who?" Mark excitedly asked as he and then Vinnie jointly realized they might have a witness to what happened that night.

"That guy who...changed right in front of my eyes," the man said with a breath reeking of cheap wine. The guy was dressed in filthy ragged clothes and was incredibly dirty. Clearly, he lived out here in the woods.

"Tell us what you saw," Vinnie calmly asked, trying to put the old man at his ease and get information. "We won't hurt you."

The homeless grey-haired man gazed warily at them. "If I tell you…if I show you too…you won't lock me up like some loon right," he said as he weaved on his feet. "I ain't going back to a loony bin again," he vehemently insisted.

"No, you have our word on that provided you tell us right now what you saw that night," Mark assured him.

"Well, I ain't seen anything like it," the man replied, now warming up to his tale. "Some young man standing on two legs over there were you was standing, all bare-assed naked. Can you imagine! Him butt naked right by my home over there," he muttered as he pointed to somewhere beyond the nearby trees. He gave the two men an indignant look then went on. "One moment standing, next one on all fours making funny noises then, BAM he's looking like some big old dog." He stopped, appearing wild-eyed at recalling what he had seen. He took out a grimy hip flask and took a long drink.

"What else," Vinnie urged, his police instinct telling him there was more to the story by just the way the man was acting in front of them.

"Well," the homeless man replied with a big smile, happy to be the center of attention for once. "These other two hooded figures shot him."

"They killed him!" A horrified Mark interjected.

"Did I say that!" the old man grumbled. "I said, youngster, that they shot him. But it was with some type of dart gun or something cause he just keels over and lays on the ground after a few seconds, breathing like he was asleep. That is when they go get him. Man, those two hooded figures just wrapped him up like a prime rib of beef. Carted him off quick, too."

"Did you see where they went," Vinnie asked.

The homeless guy merely waved his arm in a wide dismissive arc. "Out of the park, that's all I saw. All I wanted to see by then was my bottle back in my tent, let me tell you!"

"Can you describe the two hooded figures you saw," Vinnie hopefully continued quizzing the old man, eager for any further shreds of information that might prove helpful.

The old man harrumphed with annoyance. "I said they were hooded. Don't you two listen or what? Gees!" He looked at the two men, then finally shrugged his shoulders. "I do recall that one was a tall one while the other was a real runt, if you catch my meaning. I bet if I saw them, though, I'd recognize them."

"Thank you." Vinnie said as he handed the man twenty dollars. "We may ask you to do that."

The homeless man smiled. He reached into his pocket and pulled out a silver bracelet made up of a series of small tarnished engraved disks. "The runt dropped this thing," he stated as he handed it to Vinnie, "I don't take charity but a fair trade is fine, right?" He mumbled as he turned and shuffled from them back into the bushes, where he soon disappeared from their view.

Vinnie examined the unusual designs on the disk, then handed it to Mark. "Take a look at this Mark."

Mark examined the jewelry. He suddenly grew pale. "Jupiter Best And Greatest," he muttered.

"You recognize it or something?' Vinnie inquired.

Mark gazed over at Vinnie. "I know what it represents but lets not talk here. Someone is around spying on us, I'm sure of it. Lets get out of the park and go to a place we can talk in private or at least somewhere we can be sure no one else will hear us."

"As long as it includes a drink, okay," Vinnie agreed as he dusted himself off. "After my roll on the ground with that guy I need a stiff drink."

A few minutes after they left the area the homeless man heard a noise behind him. He turned, then shook with terror at the person he saw now standing before him.

"It's you! That night…it was you…taking that big dog," he babbled in fear. "Don't hurt me," he pitifully moaned as the person approached him.

"I'm surprised," the figure hissed with derision. "Didn't your parents tell you NEVER talk to strangers, especially when you are alone in a park," the person laughed a second before the figure reached out, grabbed the homeless man around his throat, then quickly and efficiently snapped the man's neck! Satisfied with the result, the person casually left the park, as well.

WHILE IN ANOTHER DARK PLACE

A still naked Jean-Claude lay huddled in the center of his cage, trying to keep warm despite the dampness of the icy room. Their massive stonewalls seemed to radiate a chilly atmosphere that by now had kept him in a state of constant unrelenting coldness. He had not eaten for days when, after he was served his first meal, his wolfish senses detected some strange substance laced inside the food and water. He had to assume that it was the same scorpion toxin they had first used on him. There was no way he would willingly aid in their efforts to keep him drugged and unable to fight back. His empty stomach growled despite all his efforts not to think of food or drink.

They had not provided him with any clothing or covering whatsoever, and by now he knew they would not do so. "I'm so cold," he thought as he tried to decide how to again adjust his body to enable him to keep at least one part of it warm for just awhile. He knew he was feverish but even his higher temperature did nothing to alleviate the effects of the freezing air on his body. The rancid vapors that emanated from the section of his cage where he had been ultimately compelled to relieve himself were nauseating. They had even refused, it seems, to take measures to take this away. The sickening smells that filled his lungs only added to his deteriorating physical state.

His current situation was maddening. Who would do this? What other person or persons in the supernatural community would be engaged in such intense black magic? After his initial encounter with the hag he quickly knew that she had to be part of some group or had another person helping her. This old woman may have been able to shoot a dart gun, but transporting him from the park by herself was beyond her physical abilities. He also had a hazy recollection of hearing separate distinct voices before he had been rendered unconscious that night. She had help, that much was clear. As he pondered all this he heard the chamber door open.

"Enjoying the nice accommodations, my beautiful young crown prince?" The old woman cackled with glee. "Ah, not touched your food again," she muttered in annoyance as she saw the plates of food he had shoved back outside through the cage's grilling. "Got to be strong, my lovely," she stated sharply. "Want you alive when we rip out your beating heart," she manically laughed. "What, still nothing to say to me again," she grumbled in annoyance.

Jean-Claude just stayed where he was in absolute silence. He wouldn't engage in further talks with her and thus waste what little strength he had left. He steadied his frame so the old woman would not see him shivering and believe he was afraid. By now he just wanted her to be gone. His head was pounding and he couldn't find a way to stay warm.

"Not looking so lovely right now are you, my lovely boy," the crone sniggered as she took away the plates. "Well, since you won't eat and by your silences you don't appear to like my company, I'll stop coming to visit you my lovely wolf-boy." Saying that she left, muttering curses in a series of words that seemed to be a mishmash of various mangled European languages.

Late in the next day a starved and a highly feverish Jean-Claude slipped into a delirious state. "I'm so thirsty, father," he moaned as an image of his father and clan leader shimmered vaguely before him. "I'm just so thirsty." His over heated body craved the liquids that he knew would not be given to him unless his captors had first chemically treated it. "But I know not to drink what they give me, right father?" He said, seeking a sign he was correct in his actions. Jean-Claude saw his father signal his understanding. In some part of his rapidly hallucinating brain he found comfort. "I will not give in, father," he hoarsely croaked through his dry cracked lips. His father smiled and nodded encouragement. "I will not give in to them, I swear, father," he mumbled to that nodding vision before finally collapsing unconscious onto the damp cage floor. His breathing grew shallow as his body struggled to stay alive.

As he lay there, now completely oblivious to anything around him, Jean-Claude never heard the cackling glee that came from a small observation slit in the vaulted upper reaches of his room. "Not so strong after all are we, my lovely boy," the withered crone laughed as she observed the handsome werewolf just lying still in his cage. "Well, as long as you are there unconscious and helpless I might as well enjoy myself by letting these old hands explore touching your youthful firm flesh once more!" She climbed down from her perch and used the spiral staircase to quickly reach the cellar's door. Silently she entered the room. She took a key from the wall, then quickly proceeded into the very cage itself. Her delighted illogical chattering filled the cold damp cellar as she leaned over the unconscious Jean-Claude. She reached out her hands toward him, soon taking her perverse delight in the sensations that filed her as her aged flesh explored the firm naked body of the young captive crown prince! As she got up to leave she suddenly smiled. She walked over to the area where Jean-Claude had relieved himself. Using her hands to scoop up some of what was there she began methodically smearing the foul substances over the body of the prone young man. "I bet you think what I serve is shit, don't you my smug werewolf," she muttered angrily. "Well, since you won't eat my shit maybe you should just wear some of your own then, my arrogant pup." When she had finished she gazed happily down on her handiwork, wearing an insane grin. Suddenly, she exploded into wild laughter as the last shred of her mind lost touch with all reality. She left the cage, locked it behind her and, left singing about her expected delight when she received: the Strega's touch.

A MEETING AND MUSINGS

Jorgen entered the outer room of Tortego's midtown office. "Is he inside?" The security chief asked one of two secretaries that worked for the vampire leader. "Can I go in?"

"He's on the phone right now Jorgen," the pretty young female vampire replied as she flashed a seductive smile at the good-looking security head. "Mr. Tortego is currently talking to Yves, the head of the Roué wolf clan, but he said to have you go in the second you arrived."

Jorgen walked past the desks of the two women, suggestively winking at the pretty secretary while pointedly ignoring the mousy plain one. He opened the intricately carved inner office's teak door and arrogantly strode inside. As he entered Tortego's room he saw the vampire's leader and current supernatural council head listening to someone on his phone. His frustration with the person on the other end was clearly obvious.

"Yes, my best vampire is on it Yves. I swear I'm as worried as you are. That boy is like a son to me." Tortego said into the phone. "I know you only let me handle this because I assured you our team would find him and get him home to you safely. Yves there is no need to threaten my organization or me. Yes I KNOW the full moon is coming up." Tortego muttered trying to stay calm during this conversation. "No one wants a war. Yves, for the love of God, please be patient. Yes, I understand. Goodbye," he finished speaking as he hung up the phone and closed his eyes. He held up his hand indicating that he needed a second or so of quiet.

Jorgen rolled his eyes at the craven way this vampire leader had been groveling to this werewolf. He glanced around at the office that was decorated with medieval saints. The whole room had a churchlike look especially with its outer windows composed of stained glass that depicted some saint or other religious themes. *Well, as they always say, you can take the vampire out of the church but not the church out of the vampire, huh,*" Jorgen thought with contempt. *"The man even dressed like some modified latter day Roman Catholic prelate,"* the blonde vampire pondered while waiting for Tortego's sign to commence his report on his actions and observations of the two persons he had tailed.

Tortego took one last deep breath, then opened his eyes. "Well, anything to report?" He grumbled as he gazed up at his head of security with a barely hidden look of desperation. "Tell me something that will help get us out of this debacle."

Jorgen stood in front of Tortego with his hands clasped behind his back and his legs slightly apart. "I followed them as instructed," he said, "I'm ready to fill you in on things they did so far, sir."

"*Sweet Lord,*" Tortego mentally pondered as Jorgen waited a sign to start his speech. "*Just like some soldier giving his commanding officer his official report."* Tortego nodded impatiently. "Go on for the love of..."

"I observed the two of them go into the Northern Woods section of Central Park. It appeared they found the exact place he was taken. I further observed them speaking to some homeless man after they conducted a search of the site and its perimeter," Jorgen droned on using a dull officious monotone voice. "This homeless man spoke with them for a short amount of time. I believe he handed them something at the end of their conversation but I could not get close enough to see what it was. I then proceeded to follow them out of the park but I ultimately lost them in the city's subway system." Jorgen stopped talking and stood silent still at attention.

"So," Tortego, now truly seething, slowly replied. "The simple fact is that you got nothing of any substance to report to me. Your insistence on permission to follow them in order to secure critical facts for me turned out to be an underwhelming disaster."

"I believe..." Jorgen began to say before being cut off by the vampire's chief.

"I have a war threatening and my head of my security, my own personal bodyguard, is a total screw-up!" Tortego yelled. "I don't need a war! I don't WANT a war! Get out of my presence and do something constructive so there is no war! DO ANYTHING to stop that from happening!" He roared at the top of his lungs.

Jorgen nodded and marched briskly out of the inner office, barely acknowledging the two secretaries as he left the vampire's headquarters. "That pathetic old Spanish bitch is terrified of a fight," Jorgen muttered once he was out of hearing range. "How I wish we had someone like the Fuhrer running things. Afraid of a bunch of disgusting werewolves. Degenerate dogs that should have been decimated not indulged."

Outside Jorgen paced, trying to get rid of the tension the encounter had given him. "Fucking Julian and his pervert human," he hissed as he recalled going with Tortego to the PI's offices. His mind suddenly recalled the beautiful young girl he had bumped into when he and Tortego had gone to see Mark Julian. His handsome Germanic features softened as the remembrance of the woman brought a smile to his face. "I think I will visit that building and see if I can find her," he decided as he hailed a cab. While the cabby weaved through traffic Jorgen again found himself resenting Tortego's lack of leadership. "In the old days," he mumbled as he sat back and let his mind wander back in time to his Germany during those heady days just before the mid-twentieth century.

Germany 1932-1945

Jorgen had been young when he first saw Adolf Hitler address a crowd. At sixteen he had slipped out of his father's house to listen to a man that some of his schoolmates had said would be the savior of Germany. From the second he heard him speak Jorgen was entranced. Unlike his weak socialist father who poetically lectured Jorgen on respecting others, here was a truly strong man who knew that only by using ruthless power could one hope to succeed.

During the elections in nineteen thirty-two Jorgen had volunteered to help Hitler's presidential campaign. He had been personally devastated when his idol lost to that old man von Hindenburg. But the ardor he had displayed in helping in that failed campaign had brought him to the personal attention of Himmler himself. When his Fuhrer at last took over the reins of power, Himmler reached out to bring Jorgen into his SS organization.

From that moment on Jorgen felt like he had been delivered from the misery of his father's world. Himmler and his men seemed to symbolize the best of Germany. As he moved up the ranks of the SS he learned that the triumph of his leader was in keeping with the will of the great supernatural forces that always protected the German people. Nazism became his religion. Hitler became his god. Himmler became his pope!

Soon Himmler inducted him into the new way of things to come. The new Reich was the ultimate earthly fulfillment of the greater dark forces of the next world. The regime would last for a thousand years under their protection. But these dark forces needed conduits in this world to aid in the supernatural's interaction with the Reich. At Himmler's direction, Jorgen and others in the SS went out to scour Europe to find items that had occult connections and bring them home to his people. It was during one such trip that he secretly traveled to the former Austrian areas currently held by Italy. There, among the simple German-speaking people of Bolzano-Bozen, he had met Helga. She was the most beautiful woman he had ever seen. True, she was of mixed blood, having a German father and an Italian mother. Still, Jorgen had to marry her. To his surprise Helga was an asset to him. Her Italian mother knew all the old legends. His twenty-six year old bride had grown up on these tales. Helga was a treasure house of stories about the practioners of the occult and the rewards they gave if they received just the right gifts. It was thanks to Helga that he was able to locate and then capture an ancient vampire to ship to Germany. This action raised his reputation in the SS to new heights. In short order he was summoned home to receive his Fuhrer's personal thanks. Naturally his half Aryan wife couldn't be revealed so he left her in her village, promising to return for her in the future. Before he could accomplish this, however, the war broke out.

The war. So many plans were delayed, then lost in that war. Jorgen found himself stationed in Berlin helping Himmler do all that the Fuhrer needed done. He rose to the top of the SS inner group and personally handled exterminating any and all subversive "fifth columnists" within Germany, including his parents. His eagerness in performing his activities and his total devotion to the cause brought him further rewards. Himmler himself secretly inducted Jorgen into the membership ranks of his own chosen latter day knights. Jorgen's proudest gift was a ring inscribed with the sign of his occult knighthood. On select special days he joined with his knightly SS brethren to perform their sacred rituals in the castle Himmler had acquired and transformed into the center of their cult. There, in their shadowy vaulted room, they placed the recently severed heads of those anointed SS Aryans who were chosen *for this honor by their genetic perfection. Together, the knights along with their high priest Himmler tried, without success, to use these heads as conduits for the dark forces to enter this world. Those were good years for him that suddenly ended all too fast.*

As Germany sank into the mire of defeats and the allies closed in, he grew desperate not to be captured, especially by the Russians. Then the dark forces seemed to step in to save him. Himmler ordered all the occult items to be destroyed, including the imprisoned vampire. The captive vampire struck a deal with the twenty-nine year old SS officer. If he was freed he would not only get Jorgen to safety, he would transform him, as well. An increasingly desperate Jorgen had jumped at the chance and the vampire was true to his word. He turned Jorgen into one of the undead and together they made their way out of a war-destroyed Germany, using the vampire network to spirit them both to Argentina. Once they arrived Jorgen killed his benefactor to be sure his past life was completely obliterated.

Decades later Jorgen, by now convinced his extremely youthful appearance would keep him safe from being considered as a wanted Nazi war criminal, sought out Helga, finally finding her in Bavaria. She, unlike him, had aged drastically, hurt by the ravages of passing time and her struggles to survive in the brutal post-war period. Even though she now repulsed him, Jorgen took her with him when he left Europe to begin another phase of his life in America. Posing as a son and his mother, the two made a new home in New York City. At times Jorgen thought of abandoning the increasingly aging woman he once married when she was a girl of twenty-five yet, from his SS training, he considered it his Aryan duty to still provide for his wife. Her presence did not discourage him however from engaging in numerous sexual affairs. Gradually Helga faded into the background of their joint lives. He continued moving toward the future while she retreated into the world of her former youth.

———

As the cab pulled up in front of Mark's building, Jorgen's wartime recollections ended. He smiled as he considered the potential satisfactions of this new possible affair with the entrancing woman he had met here only a day ago.

A Boner Book

CONFERENCES AND REALIZATIONS

After leaving the North Woods, Mark and Vinnie grabbed the number "Four" subway downtown to the Broadway and Lafayette station. Hoping to throw off anyone following them from the park they quickly grabbed a departing train on the "V" line uptown to the Fourteenth Street platform stop where they switched subways again to take the cross-town "L" to Eighth Ave. in New York's Chelsea district.

"That should throw them a curve," Mark said as they walked along Eighth Ave for a few blocks before veering off onto a side street.

"I kept an eye out as we changed lines. No one is still following us. Now you have to fill me in on that emblem and I definitely need a drink," Vinnie replied as they entered into their favorite bar. The establishment had once been just another gas station in the formerly run down but now highly upscale and still predominantly gay neighborhood of Chelsea.

Vinnie slowly let his eyes cruise the room to be sure their entrance had not caused any additional notice other than the usual stares of the patrons that men received when they entered a gay bar. He and Mark liked this place. It had become their favorite hangout to relax and unwind after the stresses of their respective work hours. There was no undue pressure from cruisers. The light blonde wooden walls with attached unobtrusive and convenient side couches in the main room gave the place a really tasteful atmosphere. Also, the bar always attracted the type of professional crowd that appealed to them both. For their purposes today it also had the asset of being just open enough to be able to see if anyone entered later who was paying too much attention to them.

"Hey guys," Sean and Paulo, the two handsome bartenders on duty, said as the men approached the bar. You couldn't get much different in looks than these two. Paulo was a big brawny guy while Sean was trimmer, though he was still in as good a shape as his coworker. Both, however, always had a smile and they gave the place a friendly welcoming ambience. "How is the family back home, Sean?" Mark asked, decompressing from the tension of his efforts so far in this investigation and needing just a short break before he filled Vinnie in on things from the past he had thought were long gone and buried.

"Mom still loves the Midwest and refuses to even think about coming out here permanently," Sean chuckled as dark haired Paulo nodded understandingly.

"So Vinnie, any hopes for me?" Paulo asked as his infectious grin brought a smile to Vinnie, who also relished this brief return to normal, as well. Mark's reluctance to talk until they were unobserved had filled him with foreboding.

"You know buddy, if he ever dumps me it will be to that smoking body of yours I'll run to." Vinnie good-naturedly said with a grin.

"So Mark," Sean laughed. "That just leaves you and me, huh!"

"Sean, if I leave him, trust me it will be for you, buddy," Mark retorted laughingly at Sean's ribbing.

"Hey guys," a pleasant and familiar voice came from behind the men.

Mark turned. "Hey Billy," he said greeting the young cute dark-haired server who worked the floor of the bar. "Is the back section empty? We need a quiet place we can talk while we have a drink."

Billy nodded. "That place is usually empty till later tonight. Just go there. I'll steer other guys away for now. Bring you your usual, guys?" Billy asked.

The two men nodded and, after a final wave to Sean and Paulo, they walked around the elliptical bar in the center room and took seats on one of the back section's couches.

A few minutes later Billy brought them their drinks: a beer for Vinnie and an Appletini for Mark. He quickly left them so they could talk in private.

Vinnie took a swig of his beer. "Okay Mark," he grimly said, placing one of his hands on the equally somber looking PI's hand. "Tell me about the design and what it means."

Mark took a long gulp from his cocktail and began his story. "It started in the nineteen thirties and it involves Hitler," Mark replied. Vinnie's eyes grew wide and he leaned back in his seat and took another gulp of his beer.

THE DARK TIMES ARE RETOLD

"To understand the bracelet and the meaning of the design it carries it is necessary to give you some critical background facts. World War Two's savagery is well known. The Nazi's activities even took the entire supernatural community by surprise. No one among us ever contemplated that this type of massive inhuman genocide could be methodically carried on by a human race. But even before the actual war's atrocities we should have known something of the potential of Hitler and his henchmen by how fundamentally obsessed they were to somehow tap into the darker forces of the other world. Forces that even the worst in our community fear to invoke.

As bad as Hitler was, and he was, I know this, his chief toady Himmler was in some regards even more dangerous to the human race. Like his master, he was also completely obsessed with a notion of Germanic power. Himmler truly believed that dark supernatural forces could be harnessed to protect the Reich from all enemies, now and in the future. To that end, Himmler, by the late thirties, was fully engaged in the goal of literally creating a new religion with him as its high priest and Adolf Hitler as its sole god. His SS were his acolytes in this creed.

In order to bring this new religion to its total fruition, his men traveled the world seizing items and even a few supernatural community members that had any connections to this "otherworld". I think he somehow hoped that bringing all these things together in one place would let him channel into things that should never be permitted to cross into this world.

In the time just before the war's beginning he chose Wewelsburg Castle to become a sort of perverted Vatican City of the darkness. He busily went about reforming this ancient structure into serving as some type of dark force magnet. I was sent to the castle by those in our community who grew concerned over what was going on. My job was to be a spy for our kind. My job was to try and find out if the danger this man posed to our safety was sufficiently grave for us to involve ourselves in this human matter.

What I found shocked, disgusted and terrified me. The man had become obsessed with knighthood and the Arthurian legends but had sickly perverted them into his own warped vision of what they stood for. His holy grail was to secure the destructive power of pure evil and not the cup of fundamental goodness that was original focus of these tales. He chose his most loyal followers with care to aid him in this obscene "knightly quest". As a mark of his personal favor, each so called "Aryan warrior knight" was given a so-called death ring as a sign of their ultimate personal commitment to his new cult.

Wewelsburg castle was altered to serve as a home and dark chapel for these knights. In one area Himmler had created a vault to hold dead heroes of the SS and their rings. But it was one specially constructed room in particular that was the pure embodiment of his evil plans. It was an area that, at first blush, appeared by its overhead inscriptions to merely be a place set aside for prayer. Instead it was an attempt by

Himmler to provide the entryway for the destructive darkness to enter into the world. The enclosure was designed around the number twelve, which somehow Himmler rediscovered held the key to unleashing these forces. Early religious wise men and women had known of the danger of the number twelve and sought to divert others from its use by imbuing the harmless number seven with mystical significance. That room even now terrifies me as I recall it. It is hard to describe its design, actually, but suffice it to say it had in the center of its floor the design on that bracelet.

This symbol was known as the dark sun of evil. It represents the opposite of light. From its blacked center you can see twelve black rays emanating out from it to a black outer circle. From that circle the crooked rays reach outward to a final black ring. It is the key to entering this world by things that must never, should never, be allowed to roam free!

Himmler was close to activating this power but he failed in one respect. Unleashing such powerful evil requires a powerful sacrifice. Himmler's sacrificial offering was the heads of twelve perfect SS Aryan men. He never realized that to invoke the supernatural your sacrifice must be of the supernatural. The war, terrible as it was, stopped Himmler's progress before he unlocked the mystery. I'd thought this all died with those men.

If the person wearing this bracelet is trying to revive that madness we are all in grave danger because Jean-Claude would surely be such an appropriate gift. What the fool or fools do not realize is that humans, even those of my own community as well, are incapable of controlling the forces that could be unleashed."

Vinnie said nothing for a long while after Mark finished. He just sat quietly beside Mark, sipping the remnants of his beer. Then he broke his silence. "You know," Vinnie observed, "it's a good thing Jaime is completely involved in that dog's case. This one we are on looks to become a situation that will get very dangerous really fast."

"You're telling me," Mark said as he took a gulp of his cocktail. "I'm happy for once she is not in any danger."

But back at the office, however, Jaime was within a few seconds of changing that very statement!

"I know this symbol," she yelled to the empty room in frustration, as the memory she wanted to visualize proved illusive. "Think, girlfriend," she mumbled. "Maybe if I ate more often I'd be better at remembering." Jaime grumbled. As she said this her mind drifted back to her encounter with Tortego and his friend. She remembered the buzz cut blonde and well-built security chief and smiled. How sweetly he had helped her up when she caused them to fall to the lobby's floor. The nice package he had in his crotch and those strong hands with the unusual ring he was wearing. THE RING! A light went on in her brain. "Son-of-a bitch!" She yelped in triumph. "I've got to tell Mark." She hooted as she speed dialed his number on her cell.

Mark and Vinnie were in the midst plotting their next move in their case when the PI's cell rang. "Jaime," Mark said grinning. "I'll bet you she has either hit a blind alley on her case or else she wants to brag about some supposed lead. Should I take it or just chill with you for now?"

"Go on take it," Vinnie laughed. "After that Nazi occult fill-in lecture you just gave me I could use a lighter touch right now in the information area."

Mark opened his cell. "Better be good, Jaime," he smirked as he listened.

Vinnie watched as Mark's smirk gave way to a shocked look, followed by a scowl, ending with an image of concern.

"Listen, say nothing. Do nothing except get over here." Mark barked with a vehemence that now had Vinnie worried over what she had said "NO," Mark yelled so loudly a few patrons turned to see what was going on.

Vinnie gazed at everyone and said loudly. "Cheating boyfriend just got caught." The other people in the bar nodded knowingly and went back to their conversations and drinks.

"Just repeat this for Vinnie." Mark instructed as he held the cell out so Vinnie could hear Jaime's voice go over once more what she had said before to Mark. When she was done Mark brought his cell back to his ear. "Get here fast. Jaime, we found a bracelet where they snatched Jean-Claude that has that same design you just described. Yes, it must be that the two cases are related in some manner. Yes he probably did snatch your friend or at a minimum knows where he is being held. Don't argue with me, just get here now!" He sternly continued before ending with, "Yes grab a cab here. See you in fifteen minutes!"

Vinnie stared at Mark as he got off his cell. He knew from what he had heard what was going on. Jaime had unwittingly discovered who was behind their case. He gazed at Mark.

"Jorgen,' was all Mark said as Vinnie indicated his agreement with that decision. They both grabbed their glasses and gulped own the liquor in them, neither one wanting to verbalize out loud the implications of all this for a few seconds more.

"More drinks, guys," Billy asked as he circled by them.

"Oh yeah," Mark muttered as each of them further contemplated the possible nightmarish ramifications of what had been uncovered.

"You think Tortego is in on this after all?" Vinnie quizzed the somber PI. "Could he want a war?"

"I fucking hope not or else we've been played. Worse, if he is in on it he may have hired me to set me – or us – up to somehow take a fall!" He muttered angrily.

Back at the office Jaime gathered her things, got on the elevator and arrived at the main floor. As she briskly walked across the lobby to get outside to hail a cab someone grabbed her elbow from behind.

"Fraulein," a strong voice said, "I'd hoped if I waited here long enough I'd find you again."

Jaime turned to come face to face with a smiling Jorgen. "Oh," was all she could manage to squeak out as the blonde good-looking security head leaned in a bit toward her face. "I've been thinking about you a lot. May I hope you, too, did the same?" He eagerly inquired.

Jaime gulped, "I haven't had you out of my mind, especially during the last hour," she replied, trying to control her racing heart to appear to him as if everything was normal in their encounter.

A huge grin came across Jorgen's Germanic features. "Ah that is good," he purred seductively. "Why don't we go to my place and see if we can give those thoughts an even better context," he whispered while leaning in close to her right ear. He kissed her earlobe and discreetly brought himself even nearer toward Jaime who, by now, was terrified she might involuntarily shudder at his proximity or continued touch. Jorgen pulled back slightly while still keeping an intimate closeness. His wide smile revealed his perfectly straight white teeth. "I think we both would enjoy that immensely," he suggested.

"*Why are all the smoking guys usually raving assholes*," Jaime thought before realizing what she was thinking. "*I've got to get away from him to get to Mark but not make him suspicious*," she mentally decided as one of Jorgen's fingers traced along her jaw-line. "*If I'm careful I might be able to use my allure to render him agreeably pliable. I just hope my vampire bastard doesn't pick it up on it, though.*" She gazed at him fixing her own eyes onto his blue ones. "Ich bin meine liebe so traurig." She murmured sexily, using her German to nicely express her regrets to him while sugaring it up a bit using the additional personal reference term of "love". "My mother is waiting for me at home."

"You speak German," Jorgen said with surprise as he moved closer toward her with delight. "You are German, ja?"

"*Great,*" Jaime fumed to herself, "*Now he's even hotter for me. Damn. Okay, I'll just tell him I only speak a bit and try again to get away.*" She smiled at him. "German, ja. Sehr wenig habe ich Angst," she sighed, faking her regret while trying to adjust her allure downward a notch. She was so scared, however, she unwittingly went into full reversal instead and hit Jorgen with a powerful shot of uncontrollable lust.

"We go to my place now!" He gushed insistently as his libido went into overdrive, "Ja! Tell mama you will be late. My car is outside." Jorgen stated firmly as he held Jaime's arm and directed her outside in a way that clearly indicated a refusal was not in the cards. "My lovely fraulein," Jorgen repeated as he felt an erotic attraction toward this human he never knew he could feel.

"Yes," Jaime sputtered in defeat, then thought of a backup strategy. "Yes, I'll call mama and tell her." Jaime pulled out her cell and hit Mark's number. Before Mark could say a word she began speaking. "Mama, this is Frieda," she yelled into the phone trying to be heard above the street traffic. "Remember that very handsome German boy I told you I met in our office's lobby," she gushed attempting not to shake while a now grinning Jorgen lead her to his car. As he opened the door for her to get in he leaned toward her and kissed her cheek.

"Your chariot awaits," he chuckled as he literally helped her get into the front seat of the vehicle.

"Well, guess who met me in the lobby just now and mama, he is taking me to his place. I tried to tell him I couldn't but he seems to have overpowered me," Jaime prattled on into her cell. "No he won't tell me where." She turned toward Jorgen, "Mama wants to know exactly where I'll be," she quizzed as she let her finger lightly stroke Jorgen's cheek to induce him to tell her.

Unexpectedly, he took her cell and spoke into it saying mysteriously. "At my castle uptown mama. The only fit place for my German Valkyrie!" He finished saying as he handed it back to her.

"Mama," Jaime nervously said into her cell. "Yes, you heard him." Suddenly she knew approximate area he lived in, "Mama, you tell Charles, yes, Charles, mama, that I won't come to see him and my sister **at that place he found**!"

Jorgen reached over and took the cell to snap it shut. "Too much mama talking. Concentrate on me now, ja? He teasing let one of his hands reach down to fondle Jaime's thigh. He stepped on the gas as the car easily drove through traffic while a terrified Jaime hoped Mark had understood that last part of her message.

———————

"Son-of-bitch" Mark yelled as Vinnie, who had also heard the entire conversation, gave Billy a fifty and told him to keep the change.

"Lets go now!" Vinnie said as he got up off the bar's couch.

"Exactly go to where?" Mark replied with a mixture of fear and frustration. "I got the Charles reference, too. It's in the Highbridge Park area, but which freaking house?'

"Tortego knows where that bastard lives or should be able to find out fast. So, we are off to see the wizard lover." Vinnie responded as he and Mark raced out of the bar and hailed a cab to midtown where Tortego had his main headquarters by St. Patrick's cathedral.

"Let's hope he's not in on all this," Mark muttered as the cabby sped through traffic toward their destination.

———————

Tortego was sitting at his desk when he heard a loud commotion in his outer office. "What is going on out there," he roared as Vinnie and Mark suddenly burst through his door, followed by the two young female vampires that served as his secretaries.

"I'm so sorry, sir, they just wouldn't wait till I asked if you were free," the pretty one said while her plainer companion nodded, obviously terrified of Tortego's wrath for permitting this unseemly intrusion.

"No time for courtesy," Mark growled as he threw the bracelet on Tortego's desktop.

The vampire leader picked up the object and examined it. "Well, not my style but next time remember that if you must give me a present I like them decoratively wrapped with pretty ribbons, as well," he sarcastically said.

"It's a fucking Nazi death sun emblem! We found it where Jean-Claude was snatched," Vinnie stated briskly. "Recognize the design. More importantly, who wears a design like it?"

Tortego re-examined the object, then a look of recognition came over him. "Jorgen's ring!" Tortego exclaimed as his head immediately shot up to stare at the two men. "Do you think he is involved in some small way?"

"No," Mark answered, "I think he planned all this to probably start a war to topple you and put him in your place, or use the chaos of a supernatural war to help recreate some sicko new Nazi regime. I think he's stashed Jean-Claude at his place or knows where he is. Right now he is driving Jaime to his place. So where does he live!"

"Yeah," Vinnie joined in, "Convince us you didn't take part in all this by helping us find this sick bastard. By the way, don't you do a background check on your people?"

"I don't need to convince you of anything, human," the shaken vampire replied with an additional undercurrent of anger. "As for doing some so called "background check," our community is similar to the French

Foreign Legion in that we do not ask about your past once you sign up."

"You fucked up, Tortego," Mark quietly replied. "He's off the reservation now and, worse for your position, he is after you. Help us find him and save your butt. Do you think that pretty speech on forgetting the past will mean a fucking thing to Yves and his clan once they catch wind of this, let alone if that Nazi psycho kills their crown prince simply to start a war Tortego?" Mark ended somberly. "He means to kill Jean-Claude if he hasn't done so yet. So the ball is in your court. Are you going to help us stop him?" The two men stared at Tortego waiting for his next reply.

"I only know he has an estate in Upper Manhattan along the border of Highbridge Park," the vampire chief muttered. "But not the exact address of where he lives." Suddenly he stopped speaking and looked over at the two now terrified secretaries. "But one of you does know! That bastard intimated to me once that he's taken one of you two there for a tryst. SO," he growled as he went into full vampire mode. "Tell me this instant!"

Both young females sputtered protests claiming their complete ignorance. Mark however, who had let his vampire senses flow, detected by the individual pulse rates of their blood that one of them was even more nervous than the other. Before he could say a word, Tortego, who must have also observed this damning fact, swiftly vaulted over his desk to grab one secretary's throat and thrust her upward against the wall. The terrified girl's feet dangled in the air as Tortego hoisted her upwards. "Speak now or I rip out your throat," he snarled

Vinnie almost moved to stop this until he felt Mark's hand on his arm. He turned to face the somber PI.

"Family vampire business, stay out of it." Mark quietly suggested in away that meant no arguments over what he just said.

After a few more seconds the female vampire gave out the address. "It's that big castle-like structure by the Harlem River…the northern end of the border of Highbridge Park," she finally squealed in terror.

"Thank you but you should have answered faster," Tortego replied as he tightened his grip further, tore out her windpipe then, dropped her twitching frame to the floor. She lay there gurgling on the floorboards in a heap, her hands futilely trying to close the gaping hole in her throat while her blood gushed out from between her fingers until she died.

"You better go now," Tortego said. "I'll summon extra help and join you when I can," he turned toward the stunning and shivering pretty young secretary. "Call maintenance to clean up this mess," he muttered as he calmly went to his desk and picked up his phone.

Outside, a shaken Vinnie just stood still for a second. "Mutha fuck," he grunted in disbelief at what he had seen. "I don't know if I can just stay quiet and let that type of thing we saw back there happen again in the future, Mark," he quietly said. "I'm a cop. I can't just stand aside while some two-bit insane despot goes all vampire and dispenses his brand of justice, okay," he finished saying as he stared at his lover.

"Vinnie, remember that Jaime needs us right now, this instant," Mark sighed as he touched Vinnie's hand. "We need to get to her fast. I swear I only stopped you because he'd have turned on you if you tried to interfere. I love you, man. I couldn't let him do that, so I'd have fought him and fighting him would have lost us time to save Jaime."

"Yeah, I know," Vinnie mumbled as he leaned in to kiss Mark. "We're cool, relax. Let's go save the girl like the knights of old!"

Mark nodded. "Well, I'll grab a New York city's version of the trusty steed. I'll hail a cab."

Vinnie tilted his head toward a parked New York police car nearby. "Too slow. I'll commander us a faster ride," he shouted as he pulled out his detective's badge and ran with Mark up to the two young cops who had just gone on their break!

A CASTLE WITH A DAMSEL, HER WEREWOLF AND A STREGA

As they drove uptown in Jorgen's car through the heavy traffic of the city, Jaime found herself unsure of how to act. Since their encounter in the lobby she had kept Jorgen in a mild form of sexual desire for her but now she wondered if perhaps that might have been a tragic mistake. Instead of her allure helping her get away from Jorgen it had only ensured that he was even more determined to have her with him. By now her mind was racing trying to decide whether a better tactic might be to stop the influence she was currently directing at him. Her problem was her uncertainty that by doing so she might find herself in a worse position with no influence over the vampire. "*God, it's like that Jimmy Durante song lyric,*" Jaime thought as they drove along the border of

Highbridge Park. *"Did you ever get the feeling you wanted to go when you had the feeling you wanted to stay?"*

In the end she remembered her father's advice that when one is holding the best hand of cards they can expect and folding is not an option, then its better to stand pat. Jaime figured if Jorgen got too frisky later on her mom's golden rule about an upper knee placed directly in the groin of the other party might prove, once more, a sex demon's best ally.

At the northern border of Highbridge Park Jorgen's car took a right turn towards the Harlem River. "Jorgen, are we going on much further?" Jaime asked hoping Mark and Vinnie were on their way to her rescue.

"My estate is just ahead." Jorgen replied, pointing to an immense stone castle-like structure that was situated on a rise in the surrounding neighborhood that bordered the park. The house was built in a way that obviously gave it a view of the river. "One of the nineteenth century robber barons built it." Jorgen boasted as he pulled into the long driveway leading to the front entrance of the place. "He imported the stones from a quarry in New Jersey and he used good German stone cutters to shape both the exterior and the interior," Jorgen said with a displayed pride. He took his right hand off the wheel and placed it on Jaime's leg, giving her a dazzling smile as well as a suggestive squeeze. "We go in," he stated as the car came to a halt in front of the twin massive oaken doors to his home.

"Its getting dark though," Jaime weakly protested as Jorgen raced around the car to open her door. "Mama will be worried if I get home late."

Jorgen took her elbow and firmly eased her out of his automobile. "Mama can wait," he replied as he led her through the doors and into the main room of the estate. "I've never felt such a strong attraction to another woman before," he mumbled as he leaned in to kiss her neck.

Jaime gazed around at the faux medieval look of the structure's main room. It was filled with flags and weapon bearing sets of armor. "I... truly interesting décor," she said hesitantly as she shivered both from the coldness of the room and the sensation of Jorgen rubbing the small of her back. "Bit on the cool side, too. How nice in the winter." She continued babbling as an increasing amorous Jorgen guided her toward a staircase that she assumed led upstairs to his bed. *"No way,"* she thought, *"was THAT happening. He may be hot but he's killed a dog and then there is the matter of Jean-Claude."* The thought of Jean-Claude finalized her resolve. She would whack Jorgen with a supercharge of her sex demon allure and then, when he was dazzled and in mindless heat, use one of the maces from the nearby collection of armor to whack him senseless. She was just getting ready to throw her "A" bomb when a cracking gruff shouting voice came from a room to the side.

"WHAT ARE YOU THINKING JORGEN!" The voice screeched.

Jaime turned to see an old woman standing in the alcove of what appeared to be a larger torch lighted chamber. Above the entryway to the door the stone arch was carved with the Latin phrase: *Domus mea domus orationis vocabitur.* Thanks to Mark's insistence that she learn his original native tongue she knew that the words roughly translated to read: My house is called the house of prayer. *"Great, he's a religious nut who also has bad taste in furnishings, too."* She sighed, still hoping to figure out a plan of escape.

"This doesn't concern you, Helga," Jorgen hissed back as he stood next to Jaime, still fondling her backside with his hand before leaning in to lightly kiss her cheek.

"Tomorrow we offer the heart of that werewolf and you bring a tramp into this house tonight!" The woman yelled as she walked further into the room where Jaime and Jorgen were standing.

"I seem to have upset, I'm assuming, your great grandmother?" Jaime said, smiling weakly at the two others. "I should go."

"YOU FOOL," Jorgen screamed at the woman. "Werewolf. You mention him in front of a stranger. You are just a stupid old woman. You and I are over, do you hear. I do not care if you are my wife, we are through!" Jorgen sputtered at her.

"Your wife?" An appalled Jaime gasped as Jorgen turned toward her at the sound of her voice. "Well, mama wouldn't like that at all!" Jaime giggled nervously as she backed away from them toward the door.

"I'm afraid leaving is not an option now, Fraulein," a grim Jorgen stated as he went up to the sex demon and held her arm. "Too much is currently at stake to let you just go. Too much of a chance of you talking and the wrong people listening," he sighed in regret as he pulled her into the center of the room.

"Listen, I work for Mark Julian and if anything happens to me," Jaime sharply retorted instantly regretting her words as she saw the look that came over Jorgen.

"You are that sex demon he employs!" Jorgen wheezed as he released her arm with disgust. "You are also a man, I'm told!"

"Oh, this is a gift," the old crone gasped as she reached out to take hold of Jaime. "Another strong sacrifice to give before we offer the big gift. A sex demon being offered is powerful magic. The albino dog was not enough, but this creature and then the werewolf will…" her voice trailed off as a strange appearance came to her eyes.

"You are both nuts!" Jaime exclaimed as she tried and failed got break the woman's powerful grip. "Yes, both of you are mad!"

"No, we are not," an enraged Jorgen shot back as he also took hold of Jaime. "You are coming with us to the consecration hall, you perversion of nature. Helga is quite right. Your beating heart will be an appropriate pre-gift."

The two of them pulled a now fiercely struggling Jaime into the room where the crone had come from. "*Guys where are you!*" A panicked Jaime screamed inside her brain!

At that moment a fast driving Vinnie was racing his commandeered police car at a breakneck speed up the East Side of Manhattan. He had full sirens and lights going as he expertly maneuvered his car through the traffic. Mark stayed quiet, not wanting to break the intense concentration of his detective boyfriend who seemed to be inhabiting some quiet "zone" of concentration as he grimly cruised past lights and cars without any pause in his speeds. "Get out of my fucking way," Vinnie yelled as he squeezed past quite a few tractor-trailers. At one point Mark closed his eyes and whispered a prayer to Mercury, who was a Roman deity who loved to race and also served as the Divine Jupiter's messenger, to get them there safely in one piece. In a time frame Mark did not think possible they arrived at their destination.

"Those doors look solid. Can you bust them open in vampire mode?" Vinnie asked as they pulled up in front of the immense oaken doorway.

Mark ran out and quickly examined them, making sure they were, as he suspected, securely bolted and locked. "I'm not sure I can," he yelled as Vinnie waited in the car.

"Then move that cute butt!" Vinnie shouted as he strapped in tight, gunned the car, and rammed the doors off their hinges, sending a shower of broken wooden panels inside the giant front room. Mark hurried in after to see Vinnie rapidly get out of the demolished car and reach to his side to pull out his gun. "Okay, locked and loaded. Let's find the girl and the wolf, okay lover," he said as he went into total cop mode. Just then they heard Jaime yelling from a side room.

As Mark and Vinnie raced towards the sounds, the former quickly took note of the inscription above that room's entryway. Recognizing it for what it was, he inwardly shuddered as the two men burst into the torch lit vault.

The room they found themselves in was amazing. It consisted of twelve columns joined by a groined vault. It had twelve window and door niches and eight longitudinal windows. The place contained long ceiling-to-floor black and red Nazi banners covering the areas that would have been just empty wall space. Suspended just overhead from the center of the vault was a large, thick golden Nazi swastika that glittered in the flickering torches. In the dead center of the floor itself was a larger version of the Nazi's black sun created in a mosaic of grey and black. Off to the back of the hall there was a simple green marbled altar with two funeral urns set upon it. Between the urns burned a flame within a bronze bowl that was held aloft from the altar's surface by two winged silver angels.

"Sweet Mother of God!" Vinnie exclaimed as he took in the sites of this place. He recognized what it was and its purpose from Mark's brief description of it in the bar but seeing it now was beyond his imagination of it.

"Sick. Just sick," Mark replied, disgusted that this vile perverse room was in his city.

"Ah guys, a bit of help," they heard Jaime yelp as she struggled with Jorgen in front of the altar. Next to her was an incredibility bizarre old woman who was waving what looked to be a large silver knife.

"The Strega's must be given her prize." She cackled as she raised her knife. "Give to them and they will give their touch to you," she screamed in tandem with a terrified Jaime who saw the knife descending towards her heart.

A loud crack filled the vault followed by a high-pitched scream. The knife fell to the floor as the old woman howled while holding a bloody hand. From the corner of his eye Mark saw Vinnie lowering his smoking gun.

"Nice shot, hot stuff," Jaime shouted as she kneed the stunned Jorgen who then doubled over while releasing his grip on the sex demon. In a flash Jaime raced first toward Mark and Vinnie then safely behind Vinnie who raised his gun ready to fire if called for once more.

"Its over, Jorgen," Mark said sharply as Jorgen stood sputtering in a rage before them while the now pitifully moaning old crone stayed by his side. The scent of her foul aged blood swept over the room.

"Not, as the Americans say, by a long shot," Jorgen howled as his eyes became dark and his fangs extended to their full length. "Those urns contain the last mortal remains of two men. It took me decades to find them and now at last I am ready. After so long a wait. I intend to sacrifice that werewolf later to the great dark forces. It will be the perfect gift. They will return my Fuhrer and Himmler from their ashes as their reward to me. With them back among us, along with my own chosen eleven fellow German vampires, we will recreate the fabled Round Table. After the coming war between vampires and werewolves we will emerge to take out the weakened winners and recreate a new Fourth Reich. This time, however, the Reich will be one in the supernatural world. All humans will then be our slaves.

"Oh, give that crap a rest," Vinnie shouted with derision. "Our grandfathers and grandmothers so kicked your ass, you sick mutha fuck. Trust me asshole, humanity will do it again!"

"My man has a way with words, doesn't he" Mark laughed while still keeping his eyes on both Jorgen and the hag.

"No, the dark forces will come once I offer them that wolf-beast!" Jorgen yelled as Mark let out his own inner vampire and prepared for battle.

"No!" The old woman shrieked, "That beast is for my Stregas. For their touch in payment to me. Their touch that will restore my youth to you." She sobbed while holding her bloody hand and rocking. "The Strega's touch. The touch of restored youth!"

"QUIET, YOU REPULSIVE BITCH!" Jorgen hollered at her. "Do you think I ever intended to let you offer that beast for your peasant superstitions? Don't be even more of a deranged fool than you are right now."

"NO," the old woman loudly screamed as she grabbed the nearby silver knife and ran out a side door near the altar. "I will kill him first and receive the touch." Before any of the men could move Jaime had bolted after her.

The three men stood in the gloomy room facing each other.

"You cannot hope to win, Jorgen." Mark snarled as they faced off for battle. "We will stop you!"

Jorgen flashed his teeth, fully baring his fangs. "You and who's army?" he mockingly asked.

"Will this one do?" Said a familiar lightly accented voice from the entryway into the hall. They all glanced over to see Tortego accompanied by ten fierce looking, extraordinarily well-built vampires. "Mind if we join you to play Mr. Julian?" Tortego smilingly said as the vampires lined up alongside a nervous Vinnie and an impressed Mark. "Oh, Jorgen," Tortego sighed, feigning indifference to the now obviously terrified former security chief. "I hope, in light of the ambience of this room," he continued saying in a voice dripping with disgust and sarcasm, "that you don't mind if I brought my friends from the Jewish and Russian contingent of our community."

Jorgen stood quietly in front of the group of men. His hands clenched and unclenched. It seemed as if time had halted for them all.

"I suggest," Tortego said forcefully, "that you rapidly drop back into a non-vampire position or I will have to let my friends do…whatever," he coughed as he waived a hand dismissively in the air.

Jorgen was silent a moment then he simply nodded. His fangs drew back inward and his blue eyes returned, then flickered in the torchlight, registering his defeat.

"Very intelligent decision I'd say," Tortego responded as the other vampires moved forward and took hold of the now demoralized Nazi. "Now then," Tortego said as he calmly strode up close to Jorgen, who by now had dropped his gaze toward the floor with its dark sun emblem. "You and I are going to have a nice chat about those eleven others. Then these gentlemen," he said glancing at his vampire contingent, "will destroy this monstrosity of a room and all it contains." The vampire leader turned to a now normal looking Mark and a still unnerved Vinnie. "Where is Jean-Claude, by the way?"

The two men quickly looked at each other. "Jaime," they yelled. Mark and Vinnie turned and ran toward the entryway to the cellar, then hurried down the narrow staircase, trying not to slip on the damp mossy surfaces of the steps.

"Do you think Jaime caught up with her in time to stop that crazy old bitch, Mark?" Vinnie gasped as he followed the PI downward on the badly lit spiraling stone stairway.

"By Apollo I hope so," Mark answered back, attempting to move with both the necessary speed but also with sufficient caution, as well, as his foot nearly lost its contact with one of the stairs thanks to the mold covering it. "Watch yourself, these stairs are dangerous. One slip and you'll fall down forward on them and possibly kill us both."

When they made the last winding turn to reach the bottom of the stairs they found the old woman lying in a heap by the cellar door's entrance. The large silver butcher's knife she had carried down with her to cut open Jean-Claude's chest and remove his heart was lodged instead deep inside her own chest. Blood oozed out from her wound to form a growing puddle on the floor where her lifeless body lay. Her now dull eyes were open and it seemed as if she was staring at something she would now never reach. Did the ancient hag, in her eagerness to sacrifice Jean-Claude, simply misstep on the slippery staircase and fall on her own knife or had Jaime done this? Afterwards Mark and Vinnie never asked Jaime how the old woman had died nor did she ever volunteer the information to either of them.

Jaime had found the key to Jean-Claude's cage on a nearby wall and was inside of it cradling the barely breathing werewolf in her arms. She had covered him up with a table cloth she had seen and was gently stroking his forehead with one hand while firmly holding one of his hands with her other one. "Hold on. Help is coming, I swear," Jaime sniffled as she rocked the shivering captive in the cold room whose putrid smells almost had Mark and Vinnie ready to gag. Jaime, however, appeared to be oblivious to anything about her surroundings other than the werewolf she was holding. "I found him naked in this filthy freezing hellhole. He has a high fever. He woke up briefly to let me know he's been starved, or rather, he refused to eat the food they had continually poisoned." She said looking at Mark and Vinnie through teary eyes. "I'm feeding him some of my sexual energy so his system won't shut down. He needs medical help fast!"

"He will get it," Tortego's voice said from somewhere behind Vinnie and Mark. "I've summoned immediate medical aid. They will arrive in the next minute. He cannot die!" Tortego muttered as he gazed around at the cellar while holding a handkerchief to his face to attempt to muffle the smells. "Please the true God, he cannot die!" He uttered, visibly nervous now.

As he took in the sight of the shaken vampire leader, Mark knew precisely why he was so afraid. If Jean-Claude died and it was known a vampire was involved, especially the head of Tortego's security squad, the consequences for Tortego were too terrible to think about.

"It will be fine," Jaime whispered as she concentrated on feeding the weakened werewolf. "I'm here. You're safe now." She took a hanky out of her breast pocket and wiped Jean-Claude's face, trying to remove some of the mess that was on it.

Jean-Claude's eyes opened slightly. He stared intently at Jaime. "Stay with me. Don't leave," he weakly mumbled as he drifted off even while tightening his grip on Jaime's hand. His shallow breathing slowly deepened and took on a regular pattern. Somehow Jaime had used her allure to hook into the former prisoner's wolfish nature, feeding it with some type of life sustaining energy.

"Never, sweetie." Jaime answered as she closed her yes and held onto him. "I'm staying, I promise." Mark watched. He knew Jaime must be projecting a strong amount of sexual energy but he felt nothing. He never truly realized until just now that she and, perhaps sex demons in general, could focus that erotic force so tightly so it would flow solely into one individual.

When the medical team arrived they hooked a sugar solution up to Jean-Claude and placed him on a stretcher. All during this procedure the werewolf maintained a firm grip on Jaime's hand. Together they left in an ambulance for the private medical facilities the supernatural community funded and staffed for their own people.

"Well, Tortego now what?" Vinnie said as the three walked out of the cellar and back up into the castle's main chambers.

Tortego's eyes darkened as he went into full vampire mode. "Now I begin the process of cleaning up." He snarled as he walked away from them with his cell phone out.

Vinnie gazed at Mark and shuddered. "I think all hell is about to break out."

Mark nodded. "That, my lover, is a vast understatement. What say you and I get out of here fast before whoever he is calling arrives. There is a pet shop by us with a cute pale yellow Lab for sale. I say it has Mrs. Castillo's name on it already. Care for a trip to there, then to Long Island? Maybe stop at your mom's, as well, to say hello?"

"What do you tell her about the person who killed her dog," Vinnie queried as they walked. "After all, she wanted the responsible parties found and punished right?"

"The truth," Mark said solemnly thinking of Jorgen's and the old woman's role in the dog's death. "We found out that the persons who were responsible are dead."

"Yes, I guess it is true even with regards to Jorgen, huh," Vinnie shook his head amazed at how that initial seemingly harmless request by Mrs. Castillo had ultimately spun itself out. Suddenly he stopped and ran his hand through his hair. "Oh shit, how do I explain commandeering, let alone demolishing, that cop car upstairs."

Mark gazed at Vinnie then directed his head back at the noisy Tortego. "I think our fearless leader can do that. He may be a despotic bastard but he does have pull at City Hall! By the way, I loved that smash in the door action," Mark winked as he groped Vinnie's firm butt.

"Macho always did turn you on," Vinnie chuckled as he bent slightly to kiss Mark's right cheek.

"Will you two gentlemen get a room!" Tortego yelled as he returned back to talking on his cell phone. The two quietly left the castle to grab a cab home. They left Tortego behind speaking on his cell phone, calmly issuing out orders in Latin to someone at the other end of the connection.

SIX MONTHS LATER

Things had turned out quite well in the end. Jean-Claude, with Jaime by his side at every step of the way, slowly recovered his health. Perhaps the most dramatic event was when, shortly after the Blue Moon cycle had passed, a pale and still visibly weakened Jean-Claude slowly made his way into the council chambers. Once more Jaime, dressed up in her best white nurse's outfit circa nineteen forty-one, was beside him helping him to his chair. The assembly chamber was packed that night and the areas reserved for spectators were filled with everyone who was anyone in New York City's supernatural community. Mark, with Vinnie, had reserved seats in front to watch as Tortego announced sweeping new reforms.

"Representation for all at every level of our government," he majestically intoned, trying, by his regal demeanor, to put the best face on things. If

reform was the order of the day, he wanted to appear to be the gracious giver of it. Nobody was fooled, however. "Soon other reforms will be announced in greater detail but there is one change that I take pleasure in announcing today," Tortego said, playing now to the community while relishing in the center stage.

"I'm happy to say Jean-Claude, my dearest friend," he said, as many there tried not to loudly guffaw upon hearing this statement, "has kindly agreed to my insistent request that he serve as my vice regent of this community."

"Gees, you gotta hand it to that vampire. When he pulls out a lie he goes for the biggest one." Vinnie whispered to Mark as the assembly and the crowd roared approval.

Mark caught Tortego's eye and smirked at the vampire leader. He knew that all these changes had been the price Jean-Claude had insisted upon to go along with the massive cover-up Tortego had arranged about Jorgen's role and, more important, Tortego's clear failure to detect it. During the last few days Tortego and some of his Spanish friends had been busy rounding up and dispatching the few former Nazi vampires that had been in on the planned coup. Jean-Claude's clan had happily helped out, as well, with the latter task, insisting on their own payback for those vampire's actions which had very nearly killed Jean-Claude. The funny thing was it was Jean-Claude's father who had insisted on his clan's participation in the "honor killings." The werewolf crown prince had surprisingly argued in vain for mercy. Mark thought he detected Jaime's kindhearted influence had come into play with regards to Jean-Claude's position on the matter. As with regards to Jorgen's fate, Mark heard he had been kept safe from the werewolves' retributions and was being held for Tortego's own personal amusement at some old castle in Spain. Mark shuddered at the thought of how Tortego, a former member of the Spanish Inquisition, would take out "his amusement" on someone who had so personally betrayed him.

One other totally unexpected additional event of note over the last six months was the highly public "coupling' of Jaime and Jean-Claude.

Their attachment to each other, which began in that dank cellar, grew during the latter's long convalescence into something stronger. Jaime had never left him during his recovery and their obvious initial attraction had blossomed into love. Of course, their crown prince dating let alone possibly mating for life (as wolves do) with a non-clan member did cause some concern within the clan. Jaime however in **her** sweet way, *for with Jean-Claude it was women that solely guided his orientation*, won the clan over. In fact, the very "mixed" nature of their pairing seemed natural for a known rebel like Jean-Claude.

The two were now seen everywhere together at all the nightspots and cultural events. The New York human and supernatural media was continually filled with pictures of her newest "golden couple". As the girlfriend of New York City's sexist and richest bachelor, Jaime found herself now setting the fashion style in clothes. The "forties look" made its predictable dramatic comeback.

"Jaime's getting married," Mark sighed as he read a blind item gossip item hinting something to this effect in one of the city's papers while in lying bed with Vinnie.

"Yeah," Vinnie yawned as he stretched out naked under the bed sheets, "Jean-Claude proposed last night. Should be a nice big affair."

"I guess he's okay with the shape-shifting thing, huh?" Mark chuckled as he put the paper down and snuggled his own bare body next to Vinnie's.

"Well," Vinnie replied as he hugged Mark close, "he told her that when you get right down to it on a basic level, he's a shape shifter too, so what the hell. Besides, Jaime gets to shift into a masculine form whenever he's up at the country estate doing his werewolf thing."

"Sounds like a good compromise" Mark said. "Should I be looking for a new secretary you think?"

"Nah," Vinnie grunted as he made himself comfortable in their bed. "Jaime may dress like she exists in the mid-twentieth century but she's a modern girl. She's staying on with you, and Jean-Claude agreed. No problems there, Mark. You know, I just thought about it," Vinnie chuckled, "Jaime might one day give birth to shape shifting, werewolf sex demons. Isn't that hilarious."

Mark just shook his head at the potential mischief such offspring could bring to the office. "Other than that unsettling worry, I'd say it's a perfect arrangement all around then," Mark responded as he suddenly made a decision.

"Yeah," Vinnie grunted as his body began to feel the sexual stimulation of having Mark's torso up against his. "Should be an ideal marriage. Jaime quietly confessed to me Jean-Claude's wolfish inner nature carries with it a super charged degree of sexuality. I think our little sex demon has happily met her match. Yep, an ideal marriage."

"Speaking of marriage and meeting someone's match," Mark sighed as he felt Vinnie's hardness rubbing against his thigh. "Let's see if we can convince the happy couple to let us crash into it. You better call your…I mean…**our** mom today. I'm thinking a double wedding yeah?"

Vinnie moved his body over Mark's to come face to face with him. "Are you asking me to marry you?" He said with a huge grin on his handsome face.

"You see any other hot guy in this bed with me," Mark laughed as he reached out to push some dark curls off Vinnie's face.

"I say yes to the first question you asked before, and with regards to that last question," Vinnie hooted like a kid as he pulled Mark up toward him. "For future reference, the only hot guy in bed with you I better ever see is me. You understand, my husband-to-be!"

Mark was about to agree but his words were lost in the deep sensual kiss Vinnie was giving him.

Author's Note

The fascination of the Third Reich and, Himmler in particular, with various aspects of the occult is a matter of historical record. Himmler in fact was known to have shared Hitler's fascination with ancient dark forces of power. In addition, Himmler was reportedly eager to recreate his own version of the "Knights of the Round Table". This man also gave out so called "Death Rings" for select SS members. The Third Reich used the dark sun symbol I've described in my book. The severed heads of dead SS men being employed as spiritual conduits, however, has only been the subject of rumor. The Wewelsburg castle does exist and provided inspiration for and hopefully an accurate description of the vaulted room of my New York City castle. The latter building and its vault is total fiction, or at least I truly hope it is. The massive and impressive Huddlestone Arch and, of course, New York City's fantastic Central Park with its Northern Woods section are all very real and I strongly urge you to visit them. The bar in my book, well, I wish you a happy exploring for that one!

Oh, one last note. Please do not attempt to make Vinnie's vampire sauce. Trust me only a vampire would like it!

THE CASE THAT MARKED THE BEGINNING

Here is a short story that came to me while I was writing my Strega's tale. It was not long enough to form the basis for a full-length book but I think it fits rather nicely into this one as a bonus. It also provides some additional background facts on my characters. I hope you enjoy it. K.C.

A Boner Book

LONDON, CLOSE TO THE TURN OF THE NINETEENTH CENTURY

"Damn utter rot," Colonel Baron grumbled as he sat in the reading room of a posh and highly exclusive London club. "Waste of bloody time, I say," he muttered to himself in disgust as he threw a letter to the ground before thinking better of his action and reaching down to pick it up.

"Problem, sir?" A young man, who appeared to be in his early to mid-twenties, asked the colonel from the nearby chair in which he was sitting.

"My nephew," the elder man said. "Back from some stupid grand tour of Eastern Europe and all he shows for it is a fascination for utter rot!"

"Utter rot as in precisely what, sir?" The young man queried, looking for something to break the tedium of the night.

The old colonel moved his corpulent frame in his chair and leaned forward. His immense stomach protruded so far out in front of his body it almost threatened to topple him over. "Vampires!" He replied with a disgusted tone. "Heard some stupid dirty Slavic peasants chattering away on the existence of such creatures. Now he believes in them and wants to write about them, if you can believe it!" The retired officer huffed in anger. "Write a bloody book on them!"

"A book, sir," the young man grinned in amusement. "A book on … vampires?"

The colonel leaned back in his chair, drawing himself up to his full height. "Yes, damnation," he mumbled, "as if anyone would read any of that rot. Write a bloody book on vampires. What next? A book on bloody werewolves!"

"Well, sir it might be a passing phase," the younger man sighed as he settled back into his chair. "Amusing thought, don't you think," he softly chuckled. "Someone writing a novel about vampires. Wonder if that might sell?" He mused.

"Damned foolish idea, sir," the colonel sputtered. "Don't think you'd indulge in such rot, eh Julian?" He grunted in annoyance. "Damn writer and a writer of complete nonsense eh what!"

"No, indeed, Colonel. I believe you would never hear me discuss the existence of vampires or the fact that they existed," Mark Julian grinned while the retired officer fumed over the fact that clearly his own nephew did not share this opinion or the other young man's good sense.

Just then an elderly valet approached the two men. The white haired man discreetly went beside Mark and handed him a note. "A young man is waiting for a reply in our lobby, sir," he softly said.

Mark nodded and then opened the note to read its contents:

Mr. Julian,

Our family is in a grave crisis and our friend, Marie de Rohan-Montbazon, duchesse de Chevreuse, explained to us how you once helped her in a crisis. May we respectfully impose on your time tonight to explain our situation and ascertain if you would be willing to help us? My son, who is delivering this message, will be happy to bring you to our home in Belgrave Square.

Your servant,

The Honorable Martin Tremain, Esq.

Mark glanced up at the club's valet. "Tell the boy I will be there shortly," he replied as he took the last sips of his brandy. *"Ah, the so lovely Marie,"* he thought with a smile. Now there was a fascinating female of immense beauty and charm. She was an intelligent member of the France's old nobility who could not resist indulging in a battle of wits with Richelieu during the later half sixteen hundreds. For her efforts she was almost unmasked as a vampire by the wily prelate and Mark had to step in to help her extricate herself from that potential disaster. *"Well, if we vampires cannot help each then whom can we rely on,"* he smirked. Mark quickly finished his brandy and rose from his comfortable seat, recalling the extremely handsome and well-formed musketeer who not only helped Mark but also afterwards joined him in some rather interesting sexual swordplay. "Don't worry, Colonel," he said as he left the old officer. "After a few of his friends laugh at his views on vampires he'll see the light. I don't foresee any so called vampire books being written in the near future."

As Mark went into the lobby the colonel glanced up at the valet. "Good chap. You won't see someone of his character going in for all that silly mumbo-jumbo about vampires. That is a level headed young man!"

"Yes indeed, sir," the old valet sniffed, thinking he'd love to be home in his warm bed instead of listening to the ravings of this old pompous windbag. "Mister Julian is quite level headed. Shall I get you another brandy, sir?"

The old officer nodded. "Damn nephew. Just like all of them on his father's side. No good ever came from the Stoker family. Write a vampire book," he huffed, "I bet it will probably take almost ten years for the fool to do it."

When Mark came into the club's lobby he found a young boy, whom he placed as probably just entering his early teens, waiting for him.

"Hello Mr. Julian, I'm here to take you to our home." The youth gravely replied. "My mother and father hope you will accept their invitation and they are eagerly awaiting the honor of your presence." He continued, trying, no doubt, to lend an ambience of additional seriousness to his task. Though slight of frame there was something about him that seemed to indicate the young man had an inner solid core of strength.

"Well, let us go then, young man," Mark answered as one of the club employees brought him his hat, coat and, walking stick. "I could use a bit of a stretch of my legs so let's skip a cab and just walk, shall we. The square is only a few blocks away." The lad quickly signaled his agreement towards Mark's plan. Together the two of them left the club and entered into the dense fog that was and still is typical of London.

"My parents are quite troubled, sir," the boy said as they briskly walked through the dense grey mists. "I'm not supposed to know but I think it is a matter regarding my uncle," he softly said.

"I cannot promise you I can help them now," Mark stated, reluctant to commit to something before he heard all the facts. The youth glanced over at Mark. His face was a mirror of his concern for his parents. Mark coughed and placed a hand on the lad's shoulder. "If I can help them, I promise I will," he replied solemnly. The boy's face lit up into a dazzling smile. "*Quite a striking young man,*" Mark suddenly thought as he examined the classical features of this youth. To his surprise he experienced the lightest shimmer of something that drew him to the lad. *"He will grow up, I'm sure, to be a magnet for the opposite sex!"* Mark mused as they walked to the boy's residence. In a few minutes they had arrive at Belgrave square which was the most fashionable area in all of London. Living here clearly demonstrated that the Tremain's were very well off if not titled, as well.

"We are here, sir," the young man said as he eagerly scrambled up the steps of a house that, like others in the square, announced to the outside world that, within its walls, a family of means existed. He rang the bell and soon a servant arrived to open the door. Mark entered the house extremely curious now as to the nature of the aid that was being sought by this clearly respectable family.

A Boner Book

THE MEETING

Mark was ushered by a middle-aged maid into a large parlor furnished in high Victorian style. Large comfortable chairs stood by a cozy fireplace who's crackling flames dispelled the chill Mark had acquired from walking through the damp fog outside. The young boy did not accompany him into the room but went up a side staircase instead. The servant indicated that both Mr. and Mrs. Tremain would join Mark momentarily.

"If you require anything, sir, that bell over by the corner of the fireplace will summon me right quick," she stated, then added, "they are kind and good people, sir. Better than any I've ever worked for and that is a true fact." She concluded before she left.

Mark stood close to the fireplace, warming himself as he awaited their arrival. He liked this house, he thought. It truly was a home. He also found himself pondering what his hosts would look like, as well.

A minute later the Tremains entered. Mrs. Tremain was a striking woman who, though short of stature, carried her trim frame in a regal yet welcoming manner. She wore her brown hair upward resting on top of her head in the style most upper class women of the day preferred. Perhaps her most striking feature was her eyes whose green hue seemed to catch the light from the fire in the most becoming way. Though she appeared to be in her early forties, Mark immediately thought that here was a woman that men, regardless of their ages, would always gravitate toward. Yet, there was also something about her that proved illusive to describe. In fact, though it seemed illogical, he thought that something about her features changed in the brief seconds since he first saw her enter. Not great changes but slight, barely noticeable ones. As he pondered this sensation, his mind's imagining were dispelled by the voice of Mr. Tremain.

"Mr. Julian, thank you for coming," the man said, extending his hand to shake Mark's.

Mr. Tremain was a man in his late forties but still well formed and quite compelling in his good looks, with light brown hair that had hints of distinguished grey on the sides. His brown eyes were warm and intriguing. His handshake was firm and his voice rather soothing. As they greeted each other Mark felt a tingling followed by a slight bump within him of sexual interest in the gentleman. Then it hit him. "I believe you are a sex demon, correct?" Mark inquired as he shook off the minor effects of the man's allure.

Mr. Tremain smiled. "I prefer the term incubus, actually," he replied. "Sorry, I sometimes forget to be sure my 'allure' factor is completely off. I hope I did not offend."

"Dear, it's never completely off," his attractive wife chuckled, giving a sly sideways look to her husband. "At least as far as I'm concerned it never is."

Mr. Tremain blushed. He coughed slightly and then a more somber visage came over him. "Mr. Julian, we need your help desperately."

"Please call me Mark," the vampire said as the man's wife guided him toward a chair.

"Lets all sit," her melodious voice said to the men. "Emma is bringing in some liquid refreshments and some biscuits. Once that is accomplished we can discuss our situation with Mark."

As they sat the maid brought in a tray that held a teapot and cups along with a cut crystal decanter, which contained a reddish liquid. Mark watched as Mrs. Tremain poured the tea, thinking whatever they were about to discuss with him must be quite painful if they were putting it off for a short time. *"Probably involving family,"* Mark decided. *"An intimate area of discussion one doesn't just rush into with a stranger, yet it must be as it lies beyond a family's ability to handle by themselves."* Mrs. Tremain poured the reddish liquid from the decanter into a wine glass and handed it to Mark. To his delight when he tasted the substance he discovered it was a fine blood type.

"I hope it is satisfactory?" The wife politely inquired. "We don't…well, we asked about and ordered from **Bartels and Bones Ltd**. I believe your community uses them as their purveyors of choice?" She waited for his reply, apparently anxious about the selection.

"No, it's a superb vintage," Mark quickly assured her, impressed by this unexpected courtesy they had extended towards him. He was rewarded by a delightful smile from his hostess.

"Well, I'm happy," she responded. Turning to her husband she signaled he should begin explaining why Mark had been asked here to their home.

After a few seconds Mr. Tremain hesitantly spoke. "Our problem is with regards to my half brother, Stefan. He is currently inhabiting a tawdry area of London." Tremain stopped and looked at his wife who nodded as if telling him it had to be said.

"My…Stefan…has lost himself in…he has gone," he again halted now, looking his wife in desperation.

She breathed in deeply, then sighed and spoke. "This is a painful subject, sir, so I hope you will indulge our reticence."

"Madam, I completely understand." Mark soothingly replied as he sat back in the chair and sipped his beverage.

Mrs. Tremain took another deep breath while her husband glanced off to one side, clearly lost in pain.

He continued where he had left off but still kept his eyes averted from directly engaging Mark's. "I'm sure you are aware that my people feed on sexual energy. It's not harmful to others and we keep this 'need' for it within certain acknowledged boundaries. My half brother, however, has…he has," he sputtered and then gazed at his wife, unable to go on.

Mrs.Tremain took up the story. "Even at an early age there was something vicious about Stefan. He didn't feed in moderation and," she paused while looking at her husband as if to express both her love for him and her resolve to lance this poison that was hurting him. "Stefan thrived, not on desires but on pain and suffering."

"I'm afraid I am confused as to what this entails," Mark queried.

At this point the husband broke in as if he, himself, needed to confront this issue. "My half brother enjoys causing pain. He feeds not on sexual pleasure but on the sensations that other give off when they are hurt," he blurted out. As if a dam had been broken, he continued speaking rapidly now. "As a boy he used his allure to allow him to ensnare a victim and then he injured them vilely to feed off the agony they suffered. My parents tried to dismiss it as something he would grow out of. When they died he came here to live with us and his addiction for it only became worse. I soon discovered he was torturing people!" He stopped and gazed at his wife who got off her chair to go over to him. Tenderly, she placed her hand on his shoulder.

"We told him this was a situation not to be tolerated," she said while reaching up to stroke her husband hair. "He even tried to harm one of us for the novelty of that type of sensation; someone who would be too young to defend themselves from such a sick attack. We stopped him and then threw him out!"

Mark looked at the distraught couple. He knew from their demeanor it was their child she was speaking of and that idea fired up anger in him. "But what need of me have you?" He asked, willing himself to be calm so his vampire nature would stay at peace for the present. "That surely resolved the matter for your family, did it not?"

"We have received news that he is now totally out of control," Mrs. Tremain said softly. "He is, we are also informed, aggressively engaged in torturing and possibly maiming helpless humans. We tried to find him but we… well, we are unused to how one secures such information from that very human class he now abuses. We were told you know how to tap into those resources and, even more than how to find him, you would know how to stop him from hurting anymore humans."

"If I do find him?" Mark said. He had already decided to help this family because they were acting not out of concern for themselves but for those their relative was preying upon. Still, he wanted to be absolutely certain he was being given a free hand in dealing with the matter.

Mr. Tremain fixed his eyes onto Mark. "If tales of what he is doing or has done is true, take whatever steps you find necessary."

A silence descended on them as Mark nodded and the husband handed Mark a drawing of Stefan. The image showed a young attractive man in his late twenties or early thirties with an appearance of something not quite sane in his eyes.

"Stop him. Do whatever it takes!" Mr. Tremain repeated as he lost his composure. He turned his head into his wife's side and quietly sobbed while she comforted him.

"Whatever it takes," the wife gravely concurred.

"The matter will be appropriately handled," was all Mark said as he rose from his seat and left the parlor.

As Mark put on his coat and hat he heard a noise coming from the stairway. He turned to see the somber young son just staring at him.

"You will make it right, won't you," the slight youth said. "They have been in so much pain due to Uncle Stefan. He tired to hurt me, you know. I didn't tell them what else he tried to do to me before they caught him that time but it…" his young voice trailed off into a silence that spoke more eloquently than any words. The boy's eyes grew red with tears that soon fell down his cheeks. "He laughs when he hurts people."

Mark's jaw tightened in anger. His inner vampire nature flared inside him as he gazed at this hurt child and imagined what his uncle had almost accomplished. "I will stop his laughing, I promise you," he answered soothingly as he walked over and placed his hand on the boy's arm. "You have my word; it ends for your uncle." Mark went to the front door and took a tight hold of his walking stick. He breathed in deeply and calmed the fires of rage inside him, saying once more for the child's benefit. "For him, it is over!" Then he went out the door to begin his mission.

THE INVESTIGATION

After leaving the Tremain family Mark hailed a Hansom cab and directed the driver to take him the section of London that the family had heard Stefan last inhabited.

"You sure you wants to go to that part of the city, guvner?" The grizzly old driver asked when he received the request from Mark. "Pardon me fer sayin so, sir, but given that a gent like you, well, sir it ain't quite safe for persons of quality, if ya gets my drift, guvner. I'd not go there if I was you!"

"No, the address is quite correct." Mark assured the still hesitant man. "I do want to go there, in fact," before then adding with a grin, "I want to go to the worst ale house there is in that area, my good man."

The driver gazed in shock at Mark. Grumbling something inaudible he snapped the reins and the cab took off.

"If he's sunk as low as the family feels perhaps the worst establishment in that area of the city may be the best place to begin to seek him out!" Mark mused, as the clattering horse hoofs and the continual grumblings of the cabby provided the only sounds in the dank fogbound night.

After twenty minutes they arrived outside a rather shabby building whose bottom floor consisted of two grimy windows through which flickering light emanated. "This is what you wanted, sir," the cabby said as Mark got out and handed him a sovereign.

"Thank you, and keep the rest," Mark stated.

The cabby's eyes grew wide looking at the very generous amount he had just been given. "Sir, if I may. I'd not be flashing this amount of money too much in there or even out here." He reached under his carriage seat to pull out a sharp fish knife. "I carries this fer protection. Have it and in good health, sir jest so you can keep safe." He gravely instructed Mark, and with a snap of his reins, he drove off.

Mark grinned at this rather unexpected token of the man's kindness. He stared at the blackened wooden entryway in the front of the building. "Well, best begin the adventure." Mark loudly laughed as he pulled on its doorknob. As the decaying wooden door creaked open he was greeted by a blast of fetid smoke that came from the lit pipes of the patrons. The smoky fumes matched the grey dense fog from which he had just left. The vampire looked around the barroom. The place was the worse kind of dive. A tawdry establishment that the cheapest whores and the most degenerate thugs called their own. There were small worn wooden tables all over. At the far end a wooden plank served as a bar counter, behind which a very overweight middle-aged woman was busily pouring out drinks. Her dirty hands matched her filthy dress.

The noise of the place had silenced when Mark first entered and all eyes turned to stare at him. "Oy, a swell!" Someone yelled out as laughter filled the room.

"Drinks on me madam. For the whole place." Mark yelled out, affecting the air of a young British lord who was out slumming. The crowd cheered and quickly everyone went back to their private conversations as Mark weaved around the inhabited tables towards the bar. If anyone looked like they'd have information it was that flabby wreckage of what once looked human, he decided.

"Oy," the female barkeep wheezed. "You better have the pounds to pay for the drinks," she grunted as a young, attractive dark-haired boy of about nineteen ran back and forth carrying drinks of cheap brown ale from the bar to the various patrons.

"Will this do?" Mark replied as he threw a gold crown onto the table.

The corpulent woman nearly fell over at the sight of the glistening coin. She instantly grabbed it and thrust it under her ragged dress between her huge breasts. She gazed at Mark with a look that indicated she was happy he was here, even as she plotted how to get more out of him. "Beggin your pardon, sir, for me manners before. I really knew you was quality," she revoltingly cooed as she put a spotty glass in front of Mark and poured some foul smelling liquid into it. "On the house young sir," she chuckled.

Mark assumed that there was something in that concoction which, if he were a human, would either render him unconscious or dead. With a smirk he grabbed the glass and gulped it down in one shot. He watched as the woman waited, enjoying her consternation when, after some time, he still stood there unaffected by the brew. "Now that we've settled all that, I've two more coins like the one I gave you for a bit of information."

The woman eyed Mark with suspicion. "You some type of fancy bobby or something?" she asked with barely concealed derision. "I don't fancy bobbies in my place. We are all respectable, ya know, in here."

"Just someone needing information and willing to pay for it," Mark replied as one of the "respectable" female patrons got up from her table and staggered over towards them.

"Seeking information about what, mister," the woman said before waving away the filthy emaciated tart that was moving closer to the bar with Mark in her sights. "GET OFF, YOU DISEASED COW!" She yelled at the whore who lurched back to her former seat at a nearby table. "Don't need her kind, sir," the fat woman softly whispered as she gave Mark a lewd wink, implying that she was more than available herself. "Now about that information you need or maybe whatever else strikes your lordship's fancy." She leaned in close and smiled wider. Her soot-stained fingers lightly touched the barely covered outline of her right breast.

Mark suppressed a shudder and merely placed the drawing of Stefan on the counter of the bar. "I need to find him, or rather, his family needs to," he said as he waited for the woman's reply. "Well, madam?"

The barkeep gazed at the picture. Mark, using his vampire's keen senses, could detect that she recognized Stefan's face by the way her blood increased its pulsations throughout her body. She glanced up at Mark. "Ain't never seen him before," she replied trying, without success, to cover the powerful fear in her voice. "Now, if you are not ordering anything else?" She paused and smiled, then huffed indignantly when the vampire didn't respond to her obvious sexual overtures, "well, then you can just go!"

"Are you sure some extra," Mark paused then continued, "compensation… might not refresh your memory." Mark slowly quizzed, unwilling to give up on his first try with the woman. Clearly she knew Stefan but was too terrified to admit it. Mark wondered why this was the situation and a part of him dreaded finding out the answer.

"I said I don't know him," she loudly insisted as her raised voice brought the room into a deadly quiet. The young teenaged boy stopped at the bar just as he was about to carry more ale to the patrons. Mark noticed him glance at the drawing and then at Mark in a way that demonstrated to the vampire some other avenues of information might be available to aid in his inquiry.

"I don't need you here, so go!" the woman yelled as she signaled three brutish toughs by a sidewall to come over.

One of the three roughly pulled Mark around to directly face them. "Wat say you and me lads here discuss how you need to listen when a lady tells you to go," he mockingly said as he moved towards Mark.

"I suggest you rethink things," Mark said calmly.

The three men began laughing. "This bloke seems to think we need a moment to think," the massively muscled man hooted in derision as he addressed his other two friends.

"Take the time to do it," Mark growled as he fixed his rapidly darkening eyes on all three men.

"Sweet Lord," one of the other two thugs sputtered as all their faces suddenly went quite pale. "Harry, we gots things to do. Let's piss off, mate." He mumbled as his other two friends quickly nodded and staggered back a few feet before finally turning and quickly leaving the bar.

Mark re-faced the shocked woman and nodded. "Well, madam, since nothing either on the bar or working behind it could possibly interest me, I'll take my leave." He grinned and moved from the bar and then turned again to look once more directly at her. "Soap, madam. I strongly urge you to consider its beneficial properties." The bar patrons broke out into loud laughter and cries of mockery as the barkeep grabbed a towel and pretended to be busy cleaning glasses. As Mark left he passed by the teenaged boy. "Outside as soon as you can," he muttered under his breath, using the guffaws to cover-up his conversation with the lad. The spry youth subtly nodded in reply. "Ten minutes, sir," he whispered softly. "I'll slip out in ten minutes."

A CONFRONTATION

Mark waited across the street for the young man's appearance. As he did so a constable approached him from out of the thick fog. "Begging your pardon, but this isn't a place to be loitering around about, sir," he said respectfully. "What with those murders going on in this area. It isn't safe, sir." He paused, ready now to come to his real issue for coming up to and addressing Mark. "I hope you don't mind me asking what a man of your quality is doing here?" Mark saw the bobby was suspicious. He was just about to answer when the youth came out of the bar and walked over toward him. The constable gazed at them both and grimaced. "I don't want none of that around my area!" He said, clearly showing what he thought was happening.

"Constable," Mark quickly said, hoping to assure the officer of the propriety of the situation while not scaring off the youth, thus losing his only possible lead in finding Stefan. "I am seeking my brother and this lad is helping me search." Mark smiled, "I surely cannot go into such places as that bar so I hired him to do it for me."

The bobby looked at them for a minute, trying to come to a decision on whether or not he should take what Mark just said as the truth. He was still suspicious but Mark was obviously a person from the upper classes and his inbreed instincts to defer to that segment of society inhibited him from pursuing the matter further. "As you say, sir," he sighed as he touched the brim of his cap and left the two of them.

"Sweet Mother Of God," the youth exclaimed after the constable disappeared in the fog. "He thought I was a rent-boy!"

Mark detected an Italian accent from the young man's speech. "Immigrant?" he asked.

The youth nodded. "I left my village near Naples. I want more to my life than to farm the land. I walked across Europe and then came here. I am working with that *puta*," he muttered in disgust as his eyes looked back at the bar, "until I save enough to pay for a ticket."

"A ticket to where?" Mark inquired. He was now curious about the lad. He realized in these few seconds he had taken a liking this dark-haired comely youth who spoke with such appealing earnestness. He wondered if perhaps the boy might be "available" for a tryst after all, but then put this pleasant thought out of his mind as he recalled his real mission tonight.

"America!" The boy replied as a look of joy came over his quite nice-looking features. "I have relatives there in a place called Brooklyn. I think it is a small village by this New York City. I go there if…" his voice grew wistful now, "she stops cheating me with my wages. She always says I owe her money for my living space under the stairs. At times she comes late at night to me to try to force herself on me." The young man said. "But I don't let her!" he defiantly stated.

"If you help me find whom I'm looking for I'll give you forty pounds which should buy you a nice berth on a decent ship leaving London for your New York City. You promise to buy the ticket tomorrow and not go back in there ever again after tonight." Mark suddenly heard himself say. He knew what that bar was like and also knew that if this young man was ever going to get away from that woman's claws it would have to be fast.

"I do not tell you for money, sir," the youth indignantly replied. "I tell you about this man because he is bad!" He lowered his voice and quickly looked around. Satisfied no one was near them, he spoke softly, "he comes here many times. He picks up the women in this place and they go off together for, you understand." He paused and grew quiet for a few seconds before continuing. "He hurts them badly, sir. He hurts them very, very badly." He repeated, as if by doing so he could convey to Mark the seriousness of this statement. "He is a violent man. Everyone is afraid of him. Over the last few months the women who went with him do not come back!"

Mark stared at the boy. "These women who leave with him, do you ever see them …" he started to say before the boy cut in.

"They never come back!" He answered gravely, his words conveying what he thought happened to these pathetic creatures.

"Do you know where he stays," Mark quietly inquired.

The lad nodded, "I saw him a few days ago when I was running beer to some good customers of that fat *puta*. He was with this street tart that lives at thirteen Miller's Court. It is just off Dorset Street in a nearby area known as Spitalfields. I have not seen him since that day but I think he will still be there."

"Thank you," Mark replied. "Take the money. Get your things right now and then go from this stink-hole to this new city at once."

The youth reluctantly took the money and then ran back into the bar. Once inside he raced to the back stairway where his bedroll was, grabbed his meager belongings and, unobtrusively, left out the back door towards the docks and a new life. Mark watched him flee and a grin of satisfaction came to his face. He squeezed his walking stick and strode off into the fog to hopefully find Stefan at this location.

The corpulent bar owner noticed the youth's absence later that night. "Curse that Italian. He went off and done a runner on me," she squawked. "Oh well, plenty more where that *dago* Pasquale came from," she mumbled as she went on working.

If Spitalfields was the foulest place in London then Miller's Court had to be the worst of the worst. The court itself was nothing more than a miniscule smelly open backyard that ran off from an alley on Dorset. The stench at the location was horrible. As Mark approached the address his vampire senses detected something more sinister mixed among the various smells. Blood, human blood, was present in the atmosphere and a great quantity of it at that. He paused to allow his abilties to center on where the odor was coming from. To his shock it was clear that the locus for it was a small brick structure bearing the number thirteen Miller's Court. It was the precise place where Stefan was last known to be living!

Mark hurried toward the domicile and opened the door. He staggered backward few steps in horror at what he saw when he gazed into the place's interior. There on the grimy bed was a woman, or what was left of her. She had been opened up and completely gutted like some large fish. Her internal organs were strewn about and the walls dripped with her fresh blood. "Jupiter Best and Greatest," Mark gasped. As a vampire he had seen killings but this was a horror beyond belief. Then he heard a light giggling emanating from a far corner of the room. When he directed his gaze over there his horror increased tenfold.

A man was sitting on the floor, drenched in blood and laughing softly as he played with a bloody object. He seemed blissful unaware of Mark's presence. He smiled at the thing he was cradling in his hands. Soon he began fondling the spongy dripping reddish mess in his grip. "So warm. So very warm." He muttered.

Mark suddenly realized what the object was. "Dear Hera, it's her sex organs!" He rasped. The other man seemed to hear this and he glanced up at the stunned vampire. All at once it hit Mark like a thunderbolt. The man before him was Stefan.

"She screamed, you know," Stefan said dully with eyes glistering in excitement. "She screamed even more than the others I cut up and killed." He laughed then licked the foul object in his hands.

"Other?" Mark compelled himself to inquire, pushing down the growing nausea inside of him. "You have done this to others?"

Stefan causally gazed over at the body. "None as good at that," he replied in an excited way that caused Mark to shudder. "They think it is only four but," he insanely laughed, "I think maybe more, actually." Stefan gazed back towards Mark with dead looking eyes. "At first it was good enough to just to feed off their pain. I so enjoyed that sensation. It is quite better than just feeding off their lusts. Then, when they knew I was killing them, that fear and panic they gave off was so intoxicating." Stefan then frowned. "But those sensations don't last long enough now so I have to do it again. This one was amazing. I must always remember to kill them slower." He sighed, "Much better to do them slower. She died slow. It was heaven, the feeding off of her. I will always do it that way now!"

Mark felt an explosive anger rising in him. "You will not do this anymore," he sharply stated, as the only possible solution in terminating this monstrosity came to him. "No more women butchered, no more of your degenerate feeding frenzies ever again!"

Stefan grinned. "I am famous, you know. I am Jack. I do whatever I want." He smugly stated. "Jack does as Jack wants. You have no power to stop me," he cackled insanely.

"No, you will not do any more of this. I do have the power to stop you, sex demon!" Mark roared as he let his vampire inner nature fully out and moved swiftly towards Stefan. "You are a mad dog!" Mark snarled as he grabbed a now terrified Stefan. "Mad dogs need to be quickly put down before they hurt more people!"

"No, you cannot stop me!" Stefan screeched as Mark plunged his fangs deeply into the sex demon's neck. "I am Jack. I am Jack!" He wailed, as if saying that name was some sort of talisman that would save him from anything of consequence.

The bloody room filled with the mad sex demon's screams for a few minutes and then a deadly silence came to the area. When what had to be done was, in fact, done, Mark spirited away the body of the sex demon. He decided not to leave Stefan's body in that butcher house in order to spare the Tremains any notoriety if later it was identified. Swiftly he and his "package" weaved through the twisted back ways of London. Thanks to the thick fog Mark was able to move unseen towards the river where he quietly dropped his foul cargo into the even fouler Thames. He slowly walked home to change his clothes while dreading his next mission: informing the Tremains of what Stefan had become and what Mark had done to end mad Jack's reign of terror!

AN ENDING THAT MARKED A BEGINNING

Mark met with the couple in the same room where they had first engaged him. He was once more seated in the large chair across from the one upon which the wife had positioned herself after Mark had been seated. Her husband was at over at his desk, gazing down at the shiny surface as if unable to face Mark. The vampire had just informed them of Stefan's death but had not yet filled in the circumstances surrounding that situation. He waited while the couple processed the tragic news before continuing his report. As he stared at the wife Mark had the same sensation that, once again, the woman looked slightly different, yet figuring out how it was so proved illusive for him.

"I'm afraid Stefan was too far gone by the time I reached him, sir," Mark slowly continued reporting as Mrs. Tremain sat in her huge chair, staring quietly in the roaring fire that gave parlor a cozy feeling completely at odds with the chilling tale the vampire was relaying to them.

"Was it truly awful," the woman finally inquired as she shifted her face toward Mark, staring at him with a look that indicated that they were prepared for the truth and expected nothing less.

Mark shifted uncomfortably in his seat. Should he go into details about what he had seen? The blood and the foul butchery of a sex demon that had clearly gone insane. As he tried to decide the husband suddenly rose from his desk and walked over to stand by his wife.

The husband placed a strong hand on his wife's shoulder and squeezed. She glanced briefly up at him with loving eyes and then raised one of her hands up to enfold his. Together they directed their attention to the vampire. "We need to know everything," he said calmly. "Leave nothing out, for the family will ask. My wife and I want them to understand the need for your actions so no questions will occur in the future."

Mark took deep breath and began his detailed report on all the things he had seen when he found and confronted Stefan. He described the carnage as the couple silently took it all in, never once interrupting to ask any questions. When he had finished the room was silent.

"It was for the best," the man's wife said, breaking the quiet of the room. She glanced from Mark back up towards her shaken spouse who gulped then nodded as he turned to a nearby table and reached for a decanter.

"You have done a great service, sir." The husband agreed. "A monster has been stopped. My God, Stefan, how could you pervert what we are in that manner," he started to sob before stopping himself. He poured a drink and brought it over to Mark. "Thank you."

Just then the sounds of high-spirited girlish giggling came from the hallway. As all three turned an excited young slip of a girl ran in, laughing in a manner that was so utterly charming that the prior gloom of the parlor vanished. "Mama, the party is tonight!" She breathlessly stated. "You promised to help me decide how to look for it." She turned her entrancing face toward Mark. "Hello, Mr. Julian," she said, summoning up a serious demeanor that soon dissipated itself behind a mischievous grin. "Did you help Papa?" She innocently asked.

"I hope I did so," Mark replied, finding her high spirits infectious. She looked familiar but he couldn't quite place her.

"Mama, the party," the young teenaged girl whined in impatience as she redirected her attention back to her mother. "I'll die if I don't look right for it."

Mrs. Tremain smiled indulgently as she rose from her chair. "If you both will excuse me." She said with an entrancing smile of her own. "It's her first party and it is being given by a rather important and socially connected family so she wants to be perfect for it. Go upstairs, dear. I'll be up there in a moment to help you."

"I understand completely," Mark said as he, too, rose from his seat. "There is really nothing more that needs to be said, so if you will permit, I've some pressing business of my own that needs my attention." He turned toward the giggling young girl. "I wish you a good time, young lady, at your event. I am absolutely confident that this party will no doubt be all the better for your presence," he concluded while simultaneously giving her a slight courtly bow.

"Oh, I do hope so," she sweetly replied as she curtsied in return in a most fetching manner before racing out of the room into the hallway. Suddenly she stopped at the foot of the staircase and turned to face Mark. "One day I think I would like to do what you do. Look into things for our community and help them," she chuckled as she faced the stairs again and hurried up them while adding, "maybe I'll even work for you doing this, as well!"

The three adults laughed as Mark went over into the hall and put on his coat and hat. "How lucky you are to have two delightful children like them," Mark replied as he took up his walking stick.

Mr. and Mrs. Tremain slyly smiled at each other as if they were amused over something Mark had not yet figured out.

"We only have one child, Mr. Julian," Mrs. Tremain said in reply. "And believe me when I say that one such child as Jaime is quite enough. But she does make a lovely girl when she chooses that form." As she spoke her features once more slightly altered yet appeared not to all at the same time.

"She, for today its her feminine form day, takes after her mother in that regard," Mr. Tremain lovingly added, putting his arm around his blushing wife while he unlatched the front door for Mark. "Goodbye, Mr. Julian," he concluded as he reached out his hand and shook Mark's.

"Mr. Julian, again my sincere thanks, also," his wife said just before a plaintive a cry came from upstairs "MAMA, the party!" She shook her head. "I really must leave you for it would be a tragedy for her if she was late to Jean-Claude Roué's party." With that she swept around and walked toward the stairs as her husband accompanied Mark to the porch and then bid a last goodbye to the vampire before returning inside to his family.

A dumbfounded Mark walked down their front stairs to the sidewalk. *"Their child is a shape shifter,"* he told himself as he sauntered towards his club, surrounded by another thick London fog. *"Her mother is one, as well. I never figured it out. Well, some investigator I am,"* he hooted in amusement. *"Investigator, hmm,"* Mark suddenly thought. *"Maybe that might be something I could do?"* He pondered. *"Surely it would stop this tedium I have experienced of late. Yes why not,"* he decided. *"Look into things for our entire supernatural community. And, a new career should be a part of a whole new start in other ways, too. Why not emigrate to that city the young Italian boy was prattling on about. Yes indeed, why not a move to New York City, as well!"* As he happily walked, content with his decision, his mind recalled the disparate images of the engaging young boy and the entrancing young girl that were one and the same person. *"I wonder what their child will be like when she goes out into the world? It is a pity I'll never know!"*

Author's note

Jack The Ripper is an actual figure. His terror is a historical fact. His killing spree happened during the late eighteen eighties. His last official victim was Marie Jeanette Kelly who lived at 13 Miller's Court, off Dorset Street in the Spitalfields section of London. It is also a matter of historical record that he was never caught nor was he ever definitively identified. Of course, this is my contribution to that speculation about whom this monster actually was.

The novel "Dracula" by Mr. Bram Stoker was published in eighteen-ninety seven. I think its safe to say our retired colonel was badly mistaken on its chances of success.

I said at the beginning of this tale, I hoped this short story provides you a bit more information on my own literary character's pasts. I wanted to give you a peek as to how my main character came to choose being a private investigator to the supernatural community. Oh, I hope you got that subtle reference, as well, to a certain New York City detective's ancestor. As for our fascinating Jaime, well what can you say, right!

THE PANICKY CASE OF THE CUCCIOLO DI LUPO

*My last Mark Julian book ended with a lighter story. I want to try to do the same here with this **very** short tale that may **or may not** take place for my characters in some distant future! Oh, <u>Cucciolo di lupo</u> is Italian for wolf cub.*

Detective Vinnie Pasquale of New York City' homicide squad leaned back in his chair enjoying the madhouse of the squad room. *"Finally"*, he thought, *"some normalcy in my life,"* he smiled reveling in the usual squad insanity around him. For the last two weeks he and his spouse Mark Julian, the supernatural's community personal vampire private eye, had been driven crazy babysitting nine-year-old Andre-Paul Roué while their parents were vacationing. It had seemed so easy Vinnie recalled when Jaime, Mark's secretary and the wife Jean-Claude current head of the Roué werewolf clan, had asked "a small favor." After all, Mark had said, they both adored Andre and he equally loved his two gay uncles even if Uncle Vinnie was just a human. "Some small favor," Vinnie grumbled. While his parents were relaxing on a second honeymoon in Italy the youngster had been driving them crazy. "Where does he get his energy," Vinnie muttered feeling every inch of his forty-two years. In truth, thanks to "the gift of eternal youth" a highly grateful shaman* had given to Vinnie, the detective still looked to be barely in his early thirties. "Oh well almost free," he told himself. Andre's parents had returned early this morning on a red-eye. They were picking the child up in a few hours at Central Park where Mark had taken the rambunctious child to let him burn up his excess energy.

As he relaxed at his desk, happy to once more be among deranged killers, his phone rang. Vinnie picked it up and immediately heard Mark's frantic voice.

"Vinnie," he said hurriedly, "I lost him. I lost Andre!"

"YOU DID WHAT?" Vinnie yelled so loudly the men in the squad room looked over. Vinnie nodded at the men and then lowered his voice. "You did what!" he hissed. "For the love of God how?"

"We were walking and we came to that section of the park by the dog run and the playground." Mark excited said. "He wanted to play so I sent him to the swings. I was sitting on the bench. I swear I had him in my line of sight and I…you know we haven't had a good nights sleep since he arrived Vinnie." Mark sputtered.

"It isn't only sleep we haven't had," a part of Vinnie's mind thought before he realized he was thinking it. "Then how did...oh no," Vinnie groaned now understanding. "You fell asleep on the park bench!" He cried in disbelief as he raised his hand to run his fingers through his hair.

"I...just a few minutes...it was warm and before I knew it I drifted... Jupiter Best and Greatest what are we going to do man?" Mark cried with a mixture of worry and terror as the thought that the boy's parents would soon be coming to meet them in just a few hours filled him with dread.

Vinnie could hear Mark was on the edge of losing it "Okay don't panic. Stay there I'm on my way!" He put down the phone. *"Oh God,"* he thought. *"Bad enough Jean-Claude finding this out but Jaime, his mother."* As he rose to leave a cop yelled out that Vinnie's mom was on line Two. Vinnie picked up the phone. "Look mom I can't talk Mark needs me fast."

"You sound upset what happened Vincenzo? You tell me now!" the voice at the other end of the phone said in a rising panic.

Vinnie, hoping to just go, finally settled on a fast explanation of the dilemma the men were facing.

"Madonna, il ragazzino," the old woman wailed in horror. "A pedophilia must have him. Sweet Jesus."

Vinnie could swear he could hear the sounds of moving air as his mother crossed herself.

"Mom I gotta go now!" He said as he grabbed his gun and holster.

"Go Vincenzo. I'll pray to Saint Jude right away," she sobbed as she hung up.

As Vinnie raced out of the office he recalled Saint Jude was the patron saint of lost causes. Did his mother think finding Andre fit into that category or was she thinking, more than likely, that it was he and Mark who fit that label?

Mark paced around in small circles as the noises of children and dogs filled his ears. "Hera please help us find him," he begged silently. "His parents will be here in just over an hour. Oh Jupiter, Jean-Claude and Jaime will kill us!"

In a blind panic he instantly decided to summon additional help. "Desperate times call for desperate measures," he grumbled as he pulled out his cell phone and dialed.

"Yes," a lightly accented voice answered. "What do I owe this pleasure too Marcus?" Tortego the vampire head of the supernatural council said in a tone of voice that was devoid of pleasure to be receiving Mark's call.

"I need help," Mark reluctantly replied while trying to appear calm during the conversation.

Tortego's loud laugh came over the phone, "Well THAT is a reversal. Usually it is the other way around." He chuckled. "So what is it that compels you to ask for my assistance?"

Mark quickly explained the situation to the other vampire. For few seconds there was silence then, "YOU LOST JEAN-CLAUDE'S SON!" Tortego screamed so loudly Mark had to pull the phone away from his ear. "First his father is kidnapped by a vampire and held under deplorable conditions," Tortego bellowed into the phone. "Now the man's son. His only child is what…kidnapped do you think or what?" Before Mark could even answer that Tortego went on yelling. "Now, once more a vampire is somehow in the center of it. War. I swear I see a war!"

"Are you going to help me find him or just bitch at me?" an overwrought Mark hollered back into the phone.

Mark Julian Vampire P.I.: The Case of the Strega's Touch

"Stay there! I'm going to come right now. Plus, I'm bringing every vampire within ten miles of that location with me to help in the search," Tortego barked as he hung up just as Vinnie arrived. Mark quickly explained what to his spouse what he had done.

"Great," Vinnie moaned as both of his hands massaged his now throbbing head. "First the kid is missing. Now my mom and Tortego are involved in this now. Gees, the fun just goes on and on!"

"Vinnie his parents will be here in less than an hour from now. What will we do?" Mark pleaded hoping Vinnie had some idea of how to end this nightmare.

"You stay here in case he wandered off and comes back." Vinnie replied as he went into his cop mode. "I'm going to start a search of the area."

For the next fifty minutes an anxious Mark prayed to every Roman god he could think of for assistance. At he end of the fifty minutes Vinnie returned alone. "This is really serious," Vinnie somberly said. "God Mark, what if Andre was kidnapped. That poor kid must be terrified."

"I'm so sorry I ever brought him here," Mark said softly. "I swear if anything happens to that sweet child…" he stopped as Vinnie hugged him.

"He will be fine," Vinnie soothingly relied. "We are in this together right, just like our wedding vows said we would."

Just then the two heard Jaime's excited voice off in the distance, "Hello you two!"

They turned to see very tan and rested Jaime and Jean-Claude strolling up to them. As usual Jaime was dressed in a couture design of the forties. The striking handsome couple waived at the now totally panicked men. As the husband and wife approached Mark and Vinnie quite a few people in the park gazed over at the attractive couple with admiring glances.

"Jean-Claude will go all wolf and rip us to shreds," Mark mumbled under his breath as he weakly waived at the pair coming towards them.

"What with this us." Vinnie grunted. "You lost him."

"Hey," Mark said turning to look at Vinnie, "Didn't you just say!"

"Babe," Vinnie replied quickly, "I'm thinking I may just, as they say, throw you to the wolves. Don't worry though because Jaime will mop the floor with me while Jean-Claude is ripping into you."

"Where is my darling boy?" Jaime eagerly asked as they came up to Mark and Vinnie, "I've missed him!"

As Mark was about to explain he was interrupted by Jean-Claude, "There he is playing with some friends!"

Mark and Vinnie spun around in the direction Jean-Claude was pointing toward. Jaime squealed in delight and raced into the dog run where a similarly eager and slightly wolfish looking young puppy immediately jumped into her arms.

"He gets his wolf transforming abilities from me but thanks to his mother he doesn't need a full moon to do it," a beaming Jean-Claude said with obvious pride as he took in their reunion. "I hope he wasn't any trouble?" he asked as a laughing Jaime hoisted up the young puppy that was exuberantly licking her face.

"No," Mark wheezed in relief. "Anytime right Vinnie."

Vinnie just nodded as the husband and wife carried their bundle of joy home so the child could transform back into human form safe from prying human eyes. "You think they might have mentioned that kid's transformation abilities to us before huh?" Vinnie groused.

As they watched the family leave the park Mark grinned and faced Vinnie. "Well all that over nothing and no one harmed by it."

Vinnie looked over Mark's shoulder. "Honey I love you," he hurried said as he backed away from his partner. "Got to run. Work right. Oh I'll let you explain it all to them honey. Remember I love you," he finished saying as he quickly turned and briskly walked toward the park's exit.

Mark looked behind him to face a highly agitated Tortego who was accompanied by thirty equally put out vampires of various ages and sexes. "Oh guys," Mark hesitantly said as they approached him. "Emergency over. Seems it was all a silly mistake. In fact this is a rather funny story actually."

> ***The Case of the Shamed Shaman***: Currently an unreported case and the participants involved in this matter are sworn never to divulge the facts. No need to shame that Shaman further.

A Boner Book

ABOUT THE AUTHOR

KYLE CICERO

Kyle Cicero is a native of the NYC metro area. When not thinking up new tales, he spends his time discovering novel aspects of gay life in the ever-changing City that he calls home. He has previously written six books of short stories and three prior novels. Most Saturdays, he can be found enjoying a frozen Appletini with his friends at their favorite Chelsea bar.

Kyle Cicero is also the author of:

- *Take Down Journeys*

- *Under the Big Top and other Tales*

- *Masterful Men of Color*

- *Masters of Asia*

- *Bound to Murder*

- *Blood Fever*

- *Blood Fever: The Misadventures of Jeremy*

- *Ghost Lovers: Tales of Seductions From Beyond The Grave*

- *Commander Cody of The Interstellar Police*

- *Ace Lewis, International Agent*

- *The Gay Daze That Is My Life*

- *B'tched: Erotic Tales of Men in Submission*

- *B'tched Men: More Tales Of Erotic Male Submission*

- *Musings in Our Gay Daze*

Available at TheNazcaPlainsCorp.com,
Amazon.com or your local Bookstore.

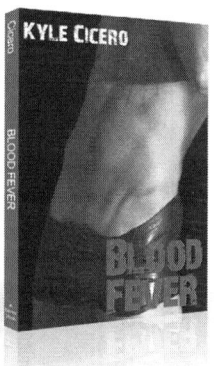
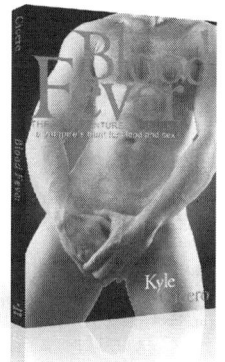
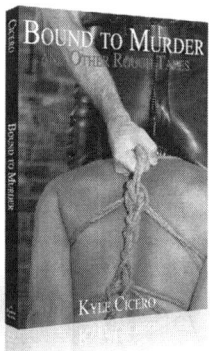

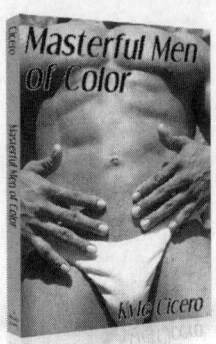

If you enjoyed this vampire book and, the Mark Julian series in general, you might want to check out another book by Kyle Cicero where he again explores the world of vampires but this time from an entirely different perspective. The following is a snippet from this work:

BLOOD FEVER:

THE MISADVENTURES OF JEREMY

Prologue:

I was born twenty-five years ago, the second son of an English lord, but was reborn only a few weeks ago being sired by a vampire whom I killed, not out of hate, but because family honor demanded it. After all, he had raped my ancestor, and in my blue-blooded family such things are not done let alone tolerated. So, my 'turned' life began in blood!

This is my journal. You may read it and like me or loathe me afterwards. Let me be honest in saying I truly do not care. You will die in time while I will not, so your opinion—good or ill—is unimportant. I write, like I act, to please myself.

Now let's begin by dispelling myths. Vampires can move around in daylight, but we prefer not to. I mean, one can hardly rip open a throat in broad daylight and not get noticed. So we stay out nights. I myself love daylight and only stay out late when the 'need' arises.

Next, crosses, holy water, the entire fantasy of religious symbols etc. used as deterrence to our attacks. Just not true. I recall one lusty young seminarian thrusting a cross into my face to ward me off. He looked so amazed when I just reached out to take it and then proceed to comment on its beautiful craftsmanship. As I bit into him I whispered to him that crosses don't affect a Jewish vampire and that he should have pulled out a Star of David instead. Of course I was joking since I'm a good English blue-blooded Church of England man myself, but I love a good chuckle, don't you?

Lastly, a vampire with any sense of class merely sups, meaning a small drinking of blood, not a full out draining till they die for you see, although we do kill, we Do not kill every time. I mean, the body count draws attention. So a nip, a bite, a command to blot out the encounter, and our victim just forgets, and life goes on for them. I rather like to think of my little tastings as similar to stopping for a nice espresso. A necessary jolt to get one going. Oh, turning others into vampires. Rarely done. Simple logic: it cuts into the food supply. We don't turn children for the simple reason no one wants to be their eternal parent. Ugly people rarely get turned as well for vampires are loath to sire ugly progeny.

And don't get me started on that whole mirrors and film crap. I mean honestly, who believes that 'they cannot be seen in or on them' silliness anyway? All cleared up now. Fine, let us proceed. By the way, I'm gay, just in case you wondered. So the old, the ugly and women are pretty safe from me. Well, unless I'm really famished. I sup on hot men but will kill the others if I'm really hungry. Vampires kill remember. Rare, but we still do it. So don't try our patience.